NEVER KISS A STRANGER

LOGAN CHANCE

Logan Chance (signature)

Social distancing doesn't mean we're not in this together...

My life is basically a romantic comedy, minus the romance and me just laughing at my own jokes.

ALSO BY LOGAN CHANCE

The Playboy Series
PLAYBOY
HEARTBREAKER
STUCK
LOVE DOCTOR

The Me Series
DATE ME
STUDY ME
SAVE ME
BREAK ME

Sexy Standalones
TAKEN
WE ALL FALL DOWN
THE NEWLYFEDS
GRAHAM

Steamy Duets
THE DECEIT DUET

***

WANT MORE SEXY ROMANTIC COMEDY READS?
Sign up for my mailing list and receive a FREE copy of
my novella RENDEZVOUS.
CLICK HERE to claim your book.

Never Kiss A Stranger

Kiki

Ellis Atwood is the devil. Ok, maybe that's too harsh. Ellis Atwood is ruining my life.

First, he demolishes a perfectly good wedding trellis.

Second, he destroys a gorgeous doggie wedding that I spent ages planning. (I kid you not.)

Third, he makes me feel all warm and fuzzy, and that is not ok. I prefer the cold and harsh way my fiancé makes me feel so much better. (wait, that didn't come out right.)

Fourth, and there is a fourth, he gets me all wound up and flustered.

And last, when he unexpectedly kissed me it made me forget my own name, or the fact that I'm getting married...in a month.

Please someone help me out. I'm a mess.

Worst part is, Ellis isn't the bad guy I first thought he was.

And being forced to spend time with him is making me realize that he needs my help more than anything.

So what's a girl like me to do?

Ellis

I'm only in town long enough to figure out a plan with my brother on how to save our brewery from the awfulness that is my father. Oh and be in a wedding.
Where I may or may not be crushing a little too hard on the bride-to-be. (spoiler alert, I'm crushing hard.)
She's really cute. Like seriously.
And she has the cutest job, she's a dog wedding planner. (I kid you not.)
I can see why Henry loves her.
I can see why everyone loves her.
I can see why I'm falling for her.
I'm usually not a relationship-type guy. Call it picky or whatnot, but usually I get bored easily. So, my plan is simple. Spend as much time with Kiki (soon to be Faniki, I know) and hopefully get bored with her adorkable smile and sexy legs that go on for miles.
Then, I can save the brewery, be the best man of the wedding, and get my butt back to Atlanta and away from the happy couple.

ONE

Kiki

NEVER TRUST A GOAT...

HAVE you ever had a goat walk all over your butt? I'm serious here. How am I supposed to stay in a zen state doing yoga as a rambunctious baby goat tramples his little hooves all over my body?

I'd never even heard of goat yoga until a few days ago when my best friend, Lola, told us about it. She's a fitness blogger and these unusual workouts are her job to find and test out. Poppi and I are the ones she ropes into coming along so she can document the fun. 'It's all for the sake of a healthier lifestyle,' she said as we entered the barn-like yoga studio earlier today.

That statement is always a bad omen. Like the time we went water walking. No, not like Jesus. This exercise involved being inserted into a human-sized hamster ball and rolled down the sandy shore into the water. Apparently, if you do it right, it's great for the abs. If you do it wrong, like me, prepare to be rescued before you drift away.

Then, there was the Thug Workout debacle which took place outdoors with things like picnic tables and telephone poles as the workout equipment. I wasn't happy about the splinters in my hand.

Lola's followers love reading about this stuff. There's nothing wrong with wanting to be adventurous while working out, but there's a fine line between adventure and just plain silly.

And maybe this is it.

I'm not complaining, because I've never been part of a yoga class where it hasn't benefited me greatly, but I just don't quite understand bending yourself into the shape of a pretzel and then thinking, 'You know what this also needs? *Goats.* Lots of little goats jumping all over us.'

Yoga with Goats. Goga? *Goga on.* Super creative title, I know. You're welcome.

"I'm pretty sure this goat just got to third base," I whisper to Lola, trying to keep my yoga pose in check.

"Focus," Lola whispers back, extending her arms forward on the blue mat. "Feel the serenity."

I blow out a breath, as a sandpaper tongue licks my heel, and attempt to relax. This is supposed to be a serene space. Soft music. Sage walls. Even the yoga teacher is the epitome of tranquility. Her name is Flower, I kid you not, and she has her purple hair piled into a wicked knot on top of her head. Other yogis would be jealous.

"Close your eyes and work through the movements," Flower purrs from the front of the class. "Now, move into the downward dog pose and don't lose your goat." Flower gives a sideways glance at Poppi whose goat took off long ago and is now nibbling on a potted plant on the opposite side of the room.

"I don't think mine likes me," Poppi says, tucking an escaped strand of auburn hair behind her ear. "And ya know, I'm not sure I mind."

My goat ambles in front of me, and I stare at his angular face while his large brown eyes stare back. "Please stay with me, little guy," I whisper as I move my body into a downward facing dog position. He hops onto my back and treks up to balance perfectly on my ass. I'm just going to ignore the implication that my butt is big enough for him to do this and savor the fact this hasn't been disastrous.

"Now move into crab pose," Flower instructs. "Keep your goat steady."

Sweat trickles down my forehead as I glance at the teacher who glides into the pose with ease, her goat looking like he's riding out the perfect wave. "Are you going to get your goat?" I ask Poppi.

"Nah, he seems pretty happy over there. I think he's divorced me." She focuses her attention back on me, not even attempting to do anymore yoga. "Speaking of, how's the fiancé?"

I try my best to keep my inner yogi at peace. "He's perfect."

That's the word my mom keeps using in her relentless texts. She's got me in some type of subliminal competition with my cousin Marsha.

"Marsha got engaged. When are you getting engaged?"

"Marsha just became Vice President of International Affairs at her firm. How's the dog grooming going?"

Marsha. Marsha. Marsha. My name should've been Jan.

I still can't believe I'm getting married, though. Me. Kiki Kingsley will soon be...ugh.

"Just the name," I breathe out, keeping my pose and goat stable. "Kiki Faniki. It rhymes."

"Kiki Faniki, the first woman on Mars," Lola says. "See it sounds more prestigious when you put it doing something important."

"But, I'll never go to Mars," I whisper back. I'm sure Marsha will, and Mom will be sure to imply I should've been an astronaut instead of opening a dog spa.

"You never know that," she says, always optimistic.

"Don't take his last name," Poppi suggests.

I shake my head. "No, my mom would have a heart attack." I close my eyes, trying to find my center of gravity as the baby goat I've named Peter tries his best to stay on but fails. He's kind of cute with his triangular black beard. He almost...no, I push the thought away. I can't even *think* it. But as he studies me with his big brown eyes, I can't help thinking...

"Oh my god, my goat looks just like Henry," I blurt out to my friends.

Lola laughs. "It's just because you're in love. You're seeing him everywhere you look."

"Be a rock for your goat," Flower says, bending like Gumby into another impossible pose.

As we mimic Flower's movements, I glance at the rock Henry proposed with. It all happened so fast.

He told me he'd never met anyone like me before, and that he knew it was sudden, but he couldn't stand living another day without me being his wife.

He said, "We don't know each other that well, but isn't that the adventure of it all? Getting to know someone as you grow old together? Isn't that what dreams are made of?"

No one had ever said anything like that to me before. I nearly died of swoon fever (It's a real condition, look it up) when he put the two-carat princess cut ring on my finger and told me his five-year plan.

He said, "Marriage. Bang. Kids. Bang. Everything will fall into place with the perfect woman by my side. Then, I'll make partner. Bang."

Me. The perfect woman.

We went home that night and made passionate love. Well, that's what should have happened, but Henry had had a bit too much champagne celebrating and passed out before any penetration took place. But, it was still a perfect night.

"This goat is infatuated with my left boob," Lola says, bringing me back to reality.

I pop open my eyes and try not to laugh as Lola attempts to keep a crab pose steady as her baby goat gnaws at her tank top. That's much more action than I'm seeing from Henry. Said the men at his firm respected values so we should wait until we're married. But, it's ok. I kind of like the idea of no sex until marriage. It's old-fashioned and romantic. Lola agrees it's very romantic. Poppi, on the other hand, said she thought maybe Henry was gay.

He's *not* gay.

He's been around all my bases, many times. He just hasn't slid into home yet.

"He thinks you're his mother," Poppi says, with a grin.

And then it's like everything takes a turn for the worse. Poppi's wandering goat tries to mount Flower, and it's seriously like goats gone wild in here.

"Ok, I think we need to regroup," Flower says.

I stop posing and Peter saunters close to nibble my palm. And then the unimaginable happens, he pretty much tries to eat my fingers and when I free my hand, my engagement ring stays behind.

Peter swallows it.

"No," I squeal. "My goat ate my ring."

I can't believe this is happening. Panic ensues for the next five minutes as Flower checks inside his mouth to no avail. I think it goes without saying we don't stay for the remainder of the class, but before we leave, I'm assured by the owner of the goats that we just have to wait a few days before I can get my ring back. Yes, you guessed it. I have to wait for a goat to poop out my engagement ring. I hope this isn't an omen as to how my marriage will go.

"Well, I think we can cross goat yoga off the list," I say to Lola as we leave the studio.

With sympathetic blue eyes, Lola loosens the bun atop her

head and blonde hair falls down in waves. "I'm sorry about your ring."

"It'll be ok," I assure her, and myself. "This too shall pass." Quite literally. "I have to go and run some errands for Georgia's wedding tomorrow. I'll keep you posted about Peter."

We say our goodbyes and before I pull away, my phone buzzes with a text from Mom.

"Marsha and your Aunt Carol are coming by for lunch tomorrow. Can you make it? They'd love to see your beautiful ring."

"Sorry," I type back, sparing her the details of my missing ring. "I have a dog wedding tomorrow."

"Dog wedding? You're not grooming any more at Dog Spaw?"

For the record, I'm not just a dog groomer. Poppi and I opened the spa, and it caters to dogs and their humans too.

"Weddings are a new addition," I reply. And pretty genius, if I do say so myself. It made sense that I give all these dog lovers something no one else can—dog weddings. I already pamper them at my doggy spa, so why not go a step further? Sounds crazy, but there's a demand. It might be a little out there, but who am I to judge? I just sat through goat yoga.

"Speaking of weddings. Marsha's having roaming peacocks." She sends a picture of an elegant peacock standing next to a white tent. "Should you check into swans? Maybe penguins?"

She sends a rapid succession of pictures to bolster her suggestion.

"No, Mom."

The wedding is already mapped out in my head. Every girl has fantasized about their dream wedding since they were young, and I am no exception to this rule. I want it to be on the beach. (You can't be from Florida and not want a beach wedding.) The turtle sanctuary near Jupiter Beach, to be exact. There's a tunnel that leads from the parking lot to the sand, and yes, I want to walk out of the tunnel like a princess walking down the aisle.

I shake my head at her competitiveness and head to Dave's Hardware to pick up the trellis for tomorrow's wedding.

This thing has been a nightmare to acquire. Who knew a white rose wrapped piece of wood would be so hard to find?

Dave's Hardware is nearly empty when I enter the store. While I wait for the salesman to retrieve the trellis from the back, I pull out my phone, checking my to-do list to make sure everything is settled for the event.

Flowers? Check.

Officiant? Check.

Chairs for the wedding? Double check.

Everything is completed. I'm a natural at this.

"Hey, Kinky," an incoming text from Henry reads. I cringe a little. We're going to have to discuss this nickname he's been using for me. For some reason, I'm not feeling this play on my name. Now, I feel I'll have to live up to it, when we finally have sex, and I'm so not kinky. "I was thinking…" he continues. "You know, Spring is my favorite season." I actually didn't know this. How can he not like Fall best? "Let's do the wedding at the Carousel."

I gasp. The Carousel is a swanky hotel and nowhere near the turtle sanctuary. "Hi," I reply. "Well, that sounds lovely, but I was thinking about the beach."

I add a smiley face to soften the blow.

My beach suggestion is swept away in a tsunami-like flood of reasons the Carousel is the best choice. Henry says he wants to get married soon, like April soon, and a beach wedding might just end in rain.

His logic doesn't squash my disappointment.

He delivers the death blow. "Sand isn't a pleasant tactile experience for me. I just can't do the beach."

Remember when I said I had my whole wedding planned out since I was a kid? Well, sometimes those ideas are childish fantasies. Sometimes, as an adult, you have to make compromises. And really, it's no big deal if I don't get what I spent my whole life dreaming about.

I guess.

No, it's fine.

Since he's picking the venue, Henry says he'll leave it up to me to choose the colors. Anything I want. Except, blue. Or green. They remind him of the beach. The fantasy I envisioned of holding a bouquet of forget-me-nots withers and dies.

My trellis arrives, and I stuff my stress-inducing phone away. Even if I can't have my dream wedding, I'll make sure the bride I'm working for has hers this weekend. Georgia will have it all, and then some.

Getting the coveted trellis to my work van is no easy feat. The cashier gave me a trolley cart to transport this thing, but it does not want to go in a straight line. I'm veering, and this trellis is leaning, and I swear it's about to fall right here in the parking lot.

"Keep it together," I tell myself *and* the monstrosity about to topple over onto the pavement.

I try my hardest to stabilize it as I zig-zag my way across the parking lot, but in a dramatic move, it comes crashing down.

Before I can even try to think of a way to get the trellis onto the cart again, out of nowhere, a car backs into the trellis with a sickening crack.

This can't be happening. But it is. My life has become a horror film starring a ring eating goat, beach fearing fiancé, and now this.

Red brake lights glow as I stare at the crushed roses beneath the sedan's tires. A man steps from the car.

"Don't you have a rearview?" I yell, as I rush to what's left of the trellis, like one would to an accident victim. I almost want to cry as I crouch next to the heap of broken wood that definitely won't be standing over a happy couple anytime soon.

"This is the day dreams die," I murmur.

Mine.

Georgia's.

Probably a million other people's. Ok, maybe not *that* many.

"I'm sorry." Emerald green eyes focus on me. They're a stunning color. Henry would hate them, because they look like the ocean. "What exactly was it?"

"It *was* a masterpiece. Pure perfection and you slaughtered it." I stand and take a good look at the murderer. And maybe I shouldn't have. This man is gorgeous—lustrous dark hair that looks like it's on the verge of a sexy rebellion and a masculine jaw that could've been sculpted by Michelangelo himself. He's what Lola would call too hot for his own good. A highly inappropriate thought forms in my mind that if I'm going with an art theme, Henry would be a Dali, all lopsided features blending together on canvas. Minus greens and blues, of course.

Dark brows draw together and the stranger's tall frame hunches over the trellis to pick up a random piece of wood. "Maybe we can fix it?"

My mind can't process his good looks *and* the disaster of the situation simultaneously, so it causes me to lash out. "No we can't *fix* it." I park a hand on my hip. "It's ruined. The whole wedding is ruined." Thoughts of telling Georgia's family that I won't have the one thing they specifically requested for her wedding causes my shoulders to slump.

The man stares at the trellis once more. "I'm sure they have more inside. Let me pay for another."

"Actually, no. This was a special order handcrafted just for my client and it took them weeks to make." His apologetic eyes sweep over my face. "It's fine. Just...leave me alone, ok?" Rude, I know. But I'm done with today.

The man glances over my shoulder and then wraps his arm around my waist. "Sorry about this," he says, closing his eyes, and slanting his lips down over mine.

He's kissing me.

Oh. My. God.

And there's some sort of misfire happening in my brain right now, because for some reason I can't seem to push him away. I can't seem to do anything. I'm going to blame my stress for the fact I haven't slapped him silly.

Yet, the way he clings to me feels so...needy. Like he can't get enough of me. His hand moves to my hair, strumming each strand, and I become hyper aware of how his tongue traces slowly over mine.

He breaks the kiss after only seconds but what felt like hours. His thumb traces down my jaw, and then over my bottom lip as if he's memorizing this very moment. And then, reality sets in— I just kissed a stranger.

"Don't do that again," I yell at him, pushing him back.

"Oh my god, I'm so sorry." His eyes are wide. "Sorry, I didn't want my..." He rubs the back of his neck as his words fall away and he just gazes at me.

That's it, I'm officially done for the day. Put a fork in me and call it. "Just forget it. You're a nightmare."

He chuckles. "I'm not a nightmare, promise. My friends think I'm a pretty nice guy." He picks up pieces of the trellis and puts it onto the cart.

I bet this guy has loads of friends. All with shining white teeth and beautiful skin just like him. I'm not normally one to notice other guys while being engaged, but this is the type of man it's just hard not to.

"Yeah, I'm sure." I gather the smooshed roses that broke loose.

He shrugs and lifts the arch of the trellis, as if it's weightless. "Yeah, they say I grow on people."

"Like a fungus? You're basically telling me you're fungi?"

The lopsided grin he gives me causes me to pause collecting flowers and stare at the slight dimple marring his cheek. "Yeah," he says. "I am a fun guy. Get it? Fungi—fun guy."

I roll my eyes with a smile. "I think that's the worst joke I've ever heard."

"Admit it. You liked it." For some reason, I feel he means more than the joke.

Rather than answer and declare myself guilty on all counts, I brush by him and dump the remains of the flowers on the trolley.

We finish clearing the ruined trellis, and he insists on loading what's left of it into my van.

As I pull away, I realize I never even asked for his name. I guess it's good I didn't.

I have a perfect fiancé.

TWO

Kiki

NEVER TRUST THE FUNNIES...

I WISH I HAD AMNESIA. All I want to do is forget about the events of today. But, that unexpected kiss is burned into my memory. I don't think I've ever been kissed like that in my whole life. I'd know if I had. And I definitely haven't.

Those thoughts are banished as I pull into my driveway, and park right next to Henry's silver BMW.

"What are you doing here?" I ask when I enter the foyer and am overwhelmed with the smell of garlic wafting through the air.

Henry smiles at me from the kitchen. "I thought I would surprise you with dinner."

"Oh, that's nice," I say, dropping my handbag on the entryway table. This is the first time I've come home to him being here. When Henry and I exchanged keys to each other's

15

places I never really expected we'd use them. I thought it was more like how Lola and Poppi have a spare key too. You know, for emergencies.

I had planned to come home, stretch out on the couch, and read a hot romance novel on my Kindle. But now, I feel like I have to entertain Henry.

Well, pretty soon we'll be married and this will be my life. You can't just get rid of your husband when you've had a stressful day. This is good practice.

I put on a smile and head into the kitchen. "Hey there." I kiss his cheek.

He wipes it away, grabbing a newspaper off the counter. "Here, I got this for you. Why don't you take it to the living room and read it for a bit before dinner."

I stare at the newspaper like he just handed me a really hard math problem. Sure, I like to keep up with the news and current events, but I haven't read an actual paper...well, ever.

"Great, ok." I take my paper to the sofa and sit between two large yellow pillows. Maybe a newspaper can be as entertaining as a romance novel.

I look at the front headline. This is horrible.

I turn the page, more bad news.

I'll look for the comics, at least those won't be depressing. Before I can get to the section, Henry sits down beside me with a few chips stacked on a plate. He grabs the business section and flips it open. And then crunches. "Dinner's got a little while before it's ready."

My eyes slide to him as he continues crunching at an extra-ordinarily loud volume.

To distract him from eating any more chips, lest I jump out of my skin, I decide to tell him about the ring. "Henry." He doesn't look up from whatever he's reading on the page, just gives a little 'mmm' sound as he licks his finger. "Today, Poppi and I went with Lola on another workout thing for her blog, and well, it was goat yoga."

He's so engrossed in his dang paper. And those chips. But, I keep going, "And well, there was this goat and he kind of ate my ring off my finger."

Nothing. No reaction.

"Henry," he glances at me, "did you hear me about the ring?"

He examines my hand. "Where's your ring?"

I stare at my ringless hand. "I just said there was a go..." Before I can finish my thought, a timer beeps in the kitchen and Henry bounds off the couch.

I follow him into the kitchen and pour myself some wine as he lifts the lid on a sauce pot.

"I had an issue with the trellis," I tell him, trying another topic. "But I think it will all come together."

He pats the top of my head, like *I'm* the dog. "That's good, Kinky."

And then I let it all out, "A stranger kissed me today, and a goat ate my ring. And also, I think I might be getting a little stressed with the whole wedding thing. My mother is just non-stop." I stare over at Henry, stirring the sauce in the pot. "Are you listening to me?"

He laughs. "Of course, I am. Manger. Goat. Blessed." He kisses my cheek. "Why don't you go take a shower? Because speaking of goats, you smell like one."

My shoulders slump, and I look down. "Yeah ok." I peer back over my shoulder before leaving. "Oh, by the way, do you have a best man yet?"

Henry's mouth disappears into a thin line. "I don't really have a lot of friends." He shrugs his broad shoulders and then his brown eyes light up. "Hey, what about that guy from your work...what's his name?"

"Dennis? You can't use Dennis. You barely know him."

"So." Henry smiles wide, reaching out his hands to take mine. "This wedding is more important to you, anyway."

Did I just hear that right? "Excuse me."

"That's not what I meant." Henry kisses my forehead. "Look, go wash the goat off of you, and then we can talk about it over dinner."

I grab my wine glass as Henry turns back to finish cooking his meal. "What are you making?" I ask before heading upstairs.

"Your favorite...spaghetti."

"Great," I tell him. Spaghetti is not my favorite. Henry asked me on our first date what my favorite food was, and I felt so on the spot, I couldn't think of anything and just blurted out the first food that popped into my head. I can't backtrack and tell him that I caved under the pressure and named a false favorite. I guess I'll have to learn to love spaghetti.

He gives me a little wave and I leave the kitchen and pad down the hallway to my bedroom.

What is wrong with me? I should be thrilled Henry is here making me dinner. But, I just wish it had been any other day than today. I need to figure out how I'm going to fix this trellis disaster, and...

I can't get the image of that stranger out of my mind.

Why would he do that? That question repeats in my head as I shower. It repeats as I eat spaghetti and listen to Henry slurp his noodles. It repeats as I finally settle into bed alone. As I drift off to sleep, I promise to myself I will never think about that stranger ever again. But, never say never.

THREE

Ellis

NEVER SAY NO...

BEER IS MY LIFE. If there's one thing you should know about me, know this...I have hops and barley flowing in my veins. And no, it's not because I'm an alcoholic. It's because my fuck-up father comes from a long line of brewmasters. My inner monologue will be continued at a later time because...

"Oh God, is that you? Ellis Atwood?" a deep voice booms from behind me.

I spin around on the bar stool and stare into the familiar brown eyes of my childhood friend from school, Henry Faniki. He still looks the same—like he just stepped off a yacht—except he's got a few smile lines and is trying his hardest to pull off a goatee.

But failing miserably.

"Dude, how've you been?" I give him a hand shake that turns into a back slap/hug thing. "Been a long time."

"It sure has. How's Atlanta treating you? Still the design genius for the brewery?"

"Atlanta's great." I offer the barstool next to mine for him to have a seat. "Yeah, I'm still running the distribution side of things."

"What brings you into town?" he asks. "Visiting family?"

"Something like that," I hedge, holding back the brewery's financial troubles Urban called me home to help fix. "Hey, I saw you were getting married a while back. How did that go?"

Even though Henry and I haven't seen each other in years, we're friends on Facebook so I see his posts every once in a while.

Henry's lips spread thin, and his eyebrows droop. "Yeah, that engagement didn't hold." His woeful expression changes to upbeat on a dime, "I'm actually engaged again, though."

"No shit. Wow, congrats." I turn to the bartender. "Mia, get my friend here the Shaggy Maggie IPA." Maybe I'm biased since I design the bottles and packaging, but it's the best on the market, in my opinion. Our IPA's are legendary. And our stouts are even better. Twist & Stout was voted top dark beer in Florida. Twice. I'd like to think it's got something to do with the bottles. Each one has a goat etched right in. Seriously.

"Sure thing," she says, before rushing off to fetch it.

"She's cute," Henry says as Mia reaches into the cooler behind the bar.

That's not exactly something an engaged man should be noticing. But from knowing Henry in high school, and the little bit I've seen on social media for the past however many years, there's one theme I've noticed with Henry's life—he sure does love the ladies.

Literally.

But people can change, right? Minus my father. That bastard will never change.

Mia slides Henry his beer across the bar wood with a smile and he lifts the brown bottle I designed to clink it with mine. "I've always loved your family's brewery." He takes a long pull of beer. "Ahh. Richard Atwood sure knows his stuff."

"That he does." I take a sip of beer, my shoulders tensing beneath my t-shirt at the mention of my father's name. What he *knows* is how to run a business that was a goldmine into a struggling mess. It's a shame, really. This brewpub has been serving the local community and building relationships with all the bars and restaurants since I was a kid.

Urban has upgraded and transformed this place into a hotspot in Jupiter. The Bearded Goat Brewery is pretty fucking cool. Behind the bar, you can see the machinery and the brewmaster mixing the hops in the taproom. People love it. Or did.

"How's your brother?" he asks.

"Urban's good," I answer. Except the high blood pressure he's developing from trying to stop the bleeding from the brewery. "So, tell me about this girl you're marrying."

He turns to face me. "She'll be the perfect little topping on my five-year plan." He takes a swig of beer. "Ever meet someone you didn't expect?"

My mind immediately travels to the woman I kissed yesterday after I picked up items to fix a broken tap. She was stunning. Long brown hair that had a slight wave, like she'd just come from the beach. Light brown eyes that lightened even more when the sun hit them just right. Curves that filled out her tight yoga pants and little top.

There was just something about her.

Or maybe it was everything about her.

I didn't plan to kiss her—I'm not some psycho who goes around kissing all the women—but it was the only thing I could think of when my father showed up out of nowhere, driving down a side street near the lot.

"How's your mom?" I ask Henry.

"She's good. Still running the gator tours." There's an awkward pause before Henry swallows down more of his beer.

"What about you? Are you still helping them out?"

"No," he scoffs, handing me a business card. "I'm an investor with a huge firm downtown. The Wright Brothers."

Ah. My ears perk up. Maybe I just found the answer to our problems wrapped up in khaki pants and blue polo shirt. I signal Mia for two more as Henry fills me in on his job and how he's making his mark on the executives by bringing in the highest potential in return investments. It's exclusive, and they invest in only the best.

"Sounds very important," I flatter him. Maybe I can convince Henry to invest in the brewery after I run it by Urban.

"Oh, it is," he assures me. "It's not as cool as what you do, artistic shit," he glances at my jeans and t-shirt, "but I like the suit and tie." He places his beer on the bar. "Can I ask you a silly question?"

"I love silly questions," I say.

"Would you want to be the best man at my wedding?"

Shocked isn't the right word for what I am right now. I haven't seen Henry in years. I don't even give his Facebook posts a like. "You wouldn't want one of your other friends?"

He shrugs. "Kiki, my fiancée, she's more into the wedding stuff." He rolls his eyes. "I just need to find someone. Anyone."

If I say yes, that's got to win me points toward an investment. "When is it?"

"A few weeks."

I pick up my beer bottle, clanking it against his own bottle. "Count me in."

"Thank God. If I had to listen to Kiki for one more second about how I needed to find somebody, I'd lose my mind."

I'm feeling a little bad for Henry's fiancée, but I laugh. "Sounds like wedded bliss."

He raises a brow. "Don't get me wrong. She's great. You want to meet her?"

"Right now?" I scan the bar, looking for a woman next to Henry that I may have overlooked.

"She's doing some wedding thing around the corner from here. We can drop in."

"Oh, no. I don't want to crash someone's wedding."

Henry laughs. "It's not what you're thinking."

"Umm ok," I set my beer down. "Let's do it."

After I settle the tab, we leave the bar and walk a few blocks to meet his soon-to-be wife. The warm sun reminds me why I loved living here as a kid. Palm trees sway in the wind as we walk down the sidewalk. I definitely didn't leave Florida because of the beauty or heat. It's a relaxed atmosphere so different from the hustle and bustle of Atlanta's big city. Everyone moves at a slower pace down here, not in a rush to get anywhere or do anything.

Reminds me of my father.

"How did you meet her?" I ask, cutting off my pesky inner monologue again.

"Dog park."

I stop walking. "Wait, you were at a dog park? Last I remember you hated dogs."

He laughs. "Oh, I still do. But, Kiki loves them. She's a pet groomer."

"I thought you said she was a wedding planner."

"Yeah, it's something new she's trying out. It's a little crazy, if you ask me."

I hate to say it, but I don't think this new engagement is going to "take" either. But that's not my business. My business is the brewery and possibly getting Henry's firm to invest.

FOUR

Kiki

NEVER TRUST A DOG BRIDE...

"LET ME GET THIS STRAIGHT. He ran over the trellis? And then kissed you?" Poppi questions, her green eyes boring into mine.

"Yes, that's exactly what I'm saying. It was absurd."

"What did he look like?" Lola asks as we stand outside the Dog Spaw, gathered at the back of my work van.

It's not important he looked like any woman's fantasy, because today is the wedding and I've got to face reality. "Just a guy." I point to the pile of wood in the back of my van to divert them away from the stranger subject. "He ruined this."

"Well, how was the kiss?" Lola jokes, clearly not dropping the subject.

There's no way I can tell her the kiss was stellar. Like a cata- clysmic happenstance that felt as if my lips were struck by lightning. No, I can't say those words, because then I'd look like a freak.

"It was ok," I finally answer, not making eye contact.

"Just ok, huh? Was there tongue?"

A bit. "No," I lie. "It wasn't like that. He just kissed me, and then went on his way, after I yelled at him."

"Wait," Lola says. "Why did he kiss you? Did he say?"

And that's the bazillion dollar question. Why would he kiss a stranger? No explanation, no nothing. And there will never be one. And good riddance. He was a nightmare. A gorgeous nightmare, but a nightmare nonetheless.

"No. He never said." I point to the pile of sticks. "Anyone know how to rebuild a trellis?"

"What are we going to do?" Poppi asks. "The wedding is in less than a few hours. Don't tell me I wore this putrid color for nothing."

The thought that Georgia's wedding could be canceled over a trellis, has me turning as green as the dress I'm wearing to match the wedding colors. We stare at the rubble as if it's going to reconstruct itself.

"Maybe we can just weave those flowers through something else?" Lola suggests, earning back friend points from not dropping the kiss. "You have a lot of doggy gates."

"Great idea. We could do something with that." With lightning speed, I remove the flowers that weren't damaged and slam the van doors closed.

If this doesn't go well, it could be the first and last wedding to take place here.

We hustle into the back of the Dog Spaw shop where we grab some gates and come up with a plan. It's a little iffy, but worth a try. Poppi and Lola get to work on the flower weaving as I check on the set up of the garden area. When I step outside into the grass behind the building, Dennis, our part-time employee, puts the last white chair in position for the guests.

Some of my anxiety fades when I see everything in place.

The sun will be the perfect backdrop to this little outdoor wedding, creating smears of pinks and oranges across the sky. I walk down the aisle. How can Henry want an indoor wedding? Weddings that take place outside hold a certain type of enchantment. The warm air delicately breezing through the veil to give that stunning appeal to the bride. Blossoming flowers standing up straight to capture the sun's rays for the best lighting on them.

"Think the weather will hold up?" I ask, moving to stand on the white wooden dais. I look up at the cloudless blue sky. "The news said a thirty percent chance of rain."

"They say that every day." Dennis rests a tan hand on the back of a chair. "It's Florida. There's always one thing you can count on...rain."

"And me," his wife, Marge says, walking up the aisle, holding a silver tray laden with bone-shaped dog cookies. "I made these. What do you think?"

"They're great. Thank you."

She smiles and slides them onto the green cloth covered table designated for gifts.

The corners of Dennis' eyes wrinkle as he smiles at his wife. That's the way I hope Henry looks at me. I try to envision Henry and I being retired like Marge and Dennis, gray-haired and taking a part-time job at the same place just to get out of the house—together. The vision never materializes. I can't picture it. Why can't I picture it? The only thing I can picture is me getting a job away from his chip eating.

I step from the dais. Marge and Dennis are marriage goals. The way he smooches her cheek when he passes by her in the back halls. The way she gets all giddy when he enters a room.

They've been married for more years than I've been alive, and it's hard to believe they haven't just met.

Poppi peeks her head out the door to call me over to check out their design. "It's no trellis, but it should definitely work."

I walk over to where the original roses now weave throughout three doggy gates. "This is perfect."

Poppi breathes out a sigh of relief and we very slowly and carefully transport it over to the podium where Dennis will stand when the bride and groom make their grand entrance.

After it's in place on the altar, I have to admit, it looks pretty damn good. The next half hour is spent tying ribbons on doggy bags, filled with goods from the spa. When I have a free moment, I check my phone for messages.

The first is from my mother—

"Marsha is hiring a string quartet for her wedding. Sounds lovely. Are you still planning on a DJ? I did some checking and maybe you need an orchestra?"

I'll get back to her later on that. Not.

The next message is from Henry—

"I'm on my way and I have a big surprise for you."

I'll be honest, I'm not a fan of surprises.

"Was that Henry?" Poppi asks. "Did you tell him about the kiss?"

"Shh. Of course, I did. It wasn't like I cheated." I whisper, like the very mention of the kiss could somehow travel through the phone and make it into Henry's ears. "I haven't even thought about it since it happened. Henry made me dinner last night and everything was...*perfect*."

Poppi side-eyes me. "That's a very long answer. Is it because you liked the kiss?"

"No, of course not," I deny.

Poppi gets that disbelieving look in her eyes she always gets whenever I talk about how romantic Henry is.

Thankfully the interrogation ends because Darlene, mother of the bride, saunters down the aisle in a tight red dress finished off with classy stilettos and pearls. "It's almost time," she says, her bleached blonde hair waving in the breeze. "The beautiful bride is here."

Georgia trails behind her, wearing a veil that was handmade to fit her ears.

"Adorable," I tell her. I glance at the time on my phone. "The photographer should be here any minute."

"Fun, right?" Poppi says to Darlene. "Why don't we go inside and get Georgia ready."

"She already looks amazing," I bend over and give her a pat on the head. "Ace is a lucky dog."

When I rise, over Darlene's shoulder, I see what must be a mirage.

I blink.

It's still there.

He's still there.

The stranger that kissed me stands at the end of the aisle, staring straight at me.

FIVE

Ellis

NEVER TRUST YOUR INSTINCTS...

I'LL BE DAMNED. There she is, looking prettier than ever in an olive-green strappy sundress with a white flower in her hair. Wow, it's almost like one of those slo-mo things, where the girl stands there smiling and you realize yes, she's the one I've been looking for.

Except, this girl isn't smiling. And that's getting way ahead of myself. I mean, we don't even know each other.

Before I can cut off this internal monologue, and make an attempt to talk to her, she's whisked away by two girls, and Henry finishes his phone call, and directs me into a row of chairs in the back. "Here is good," he says.

"I feel weird about crashing a wedding. I don't even know the bride or groom," I whisper to Henry.

Henry rolls his eyes. "Trust me, it'll be fine."

People sporadically filter in, until all the seats are filled. I'm guessing the bride and groom are pet lovers, based on the amount of guests who brought their dogs. A silver-haired man, wearing a tuxedo t-shirt and jeans, steps onto the platform in front of us, and a schnauzer soon joins him. A chihuahua licks my ankle as a bridal march pipes into the area.

All heads turn, and I follow suit, waiting for the bride to walk down the aisle.

Wait.

What?

"Umm, it's a dog," I whisper to Henry.

"Kiki has this vision that she thinks owners will love seeing their pets get married. This is her first one." His tone implies his fiancée is ridiculous for thinking this way.

But, I'm *so* on board with it.

I watch as the English bulldog is led up the aisle on a leash by a tall, older woman with platinum blonde hair toward a black schnauzer looking dog. The owner of the schnauzer smiles, and slips the black dog a treat.

This is wild.

"I have to get a better look," I tell Henry before standing. It's not every day you're invited to a dog wedding.

And it's not every day someone pulls off something so amazing.

So as not to disrupt the ceremony, I slip up the side on the outside perimeter.

The English bulldog sits at the front with a look of 'help' written all over her smooshed face.

Like this is downright the coolest shit I've ever seen. If I have one critique, they needed a trellis, because...oh...

Standing right next to me is her.

The her.

The woman whose trellis I accidentally backed into and ...what did she call it? Murdered it.

"Cute, right?" she says before landing those stellar brown

eyes on me. I can see all the different emotions play out across her stunning face. Surprise. Shock. Anger.

"What are you doing here?" she whisper-yells at me.

"I'm just here for a wedding." I smile, loving the tinge of pink splayed across her cheeks.

"Who invited you?"

"Maybe the bride invited me."

"She didn't."

"How do you know? The bride personally told you she didn't?" I raise a brow.

She huffs a little, pushing back a stray strand of brown hair that's fallen into her eyes. "You don't know the bride."

I lean in, so not to be overheard by the wedding that is in full swing now. "I was invited to the puptials. And be quiet, I don't want to miss the bride saying her bow-vows."

She parks a hand on her hip, her anger intensifying. "If you and the bride are such great friends, what's her name?"

I blink.

"Exactly. You need to leave."

"You can't kick me out of this wedding."

"I can and I will. It's *my* wedding."

I glance around, spotting a sign with a picture of the two dogs with their names underneath. "Georgia and Ace wouldn't like it if I got kicked out."

"Please leave."

I fold my arms and lean against the back wall. "Can't, I'm here to meet someone."

Her eyes study me for a moment, and then she stalks away after a tense 'fine' from her lips.

Her ass sways in a hypnotizing way underneath the fabric of her little dress. She's hands down the hottest girl at this wedding. And yes, she's even hotter than the bride. Ha. I love a dog wedding.

Can't wait for the reception. This time, I won't make the same mistake twice—I'll make sure I get her number, and name.

I head back to my seat next to Henry and watch as the two dogs are bound in holy *mutt*-rimony.

I survey the nice little crowd here today, wondering who Henry's fiancée is. Maybe one of the girls from earlier.

Knowing Henry, it's the blonde. He always did have a thing for blondes with blue eyes. He used to call them the best kind of eye-candy growing up.

As Ace sniffs his new bride's butt, I make a beeline straight for the girl, forgetting all about meeting Henry's fiancée.

He'll understand.

"I didn't see them kiss," I tell the hot little temptress who I still don't have a name for.

"You're still here?" She looks flustered, like she's trying to keep control over some sort of a chaotic event I'm unaware of. "And speaking of kissing," she turns on me, her finger waving in my face, "why did you kiss me anyway?"

"There you are," Henry belts from a few feet away. Only he's not talking about me though. To my horror, he wraps his arm around the girl *I* kissed and kisses her on the cheek. "I see you found your surprise."

Surprise?

"I finally found a best man." He's all smiles and cheers and winks and cheers again. Fuck. He's the exact opposite of how I'm feeling right now.

No, no. Say it isn't so. This gorgeous woman can *not* be his fiancée.

I mean, sure Henry's a good-looking dude, I guess. I'm sure he could score someone as hot as her, but she doesn't seem like his type...*at all*.

And I'm not being biased about that.

"This is Ellis," he says, and I try to force the muscles in my face to smile back.

"Nice to meet you." I hold out my hand, somehow keeping my cool together. "Where's your ring?" Rude question to blurt out, I know, but she did *not* have a ring on the other day in the

NEVER KISS A STRANGER

parking lot. I would have noticed. And I would have *never* kissed a woman sporting a rock on her finger. I'm not that kind of guy.

She glances at her left hand, like she too forgot she isn't wearing one. "I'm waiting on a goat to...never mind." She waves off the question and shakes my outstretched hand. "It's so nice to meet you...uh...Ellis."

Henry squeezes her tighter with a laugh, puffing out his chest with pride. "This is *my* Kiki. The affianced. She planned this crazy thing." He raises a brow at me. "Thinks it'll take off."

For some reason, I'm not liking the condescending vibe coming from Henry's eyebrow about the wedding she put together.

"You did a great job," I tell her, not letting go of her soft hand. I'm very aware that I need to because we're just standing here with our hands connected. "I think Georgia and Ace will live a long and happy life together."

Henry laughs. "She gets a lot of crazy ideas. Just the other day she was looking into llamas."

"Llamas?" Let go of her hand. Dude. "That sounds interesting."

She's not pulling away her hand either. "It was goats."

A blonde with a little white furball in her hands joins our awkward conversation.

"We have an issue," she says to Kiki, and then glances at our hands *still* joined together and eyes me up and down.

This is the moment I should definitely let go of her hand, but I swear it's like there's superglue keeping them together.

Finally, Kiki let's go, and I slide both my hands in my pockets. Don't want that happening again.

Kiki and the blonde leave, and I'm left standing here with Henry. Lucky, lucky Henry. Lucky fucking Henry. *The affianced.*

So, that was Kiki.

He smiles, like he's the happiest man in the world. And why wouldn't he be? He's got the girl. And she's a phenomenal kisser. I'd never tell him that, though.

Oh god, I've kissed his soon-to-be wife. This isn't good.

Well, I'm not telling him. And I'm pretty sure Kiki hasn't said anything to him either.

That's best. It'll just be our own little secret. Not that it was anything major. It was just a kiss. A scorchingly hot, *meaningless* kiss.

My phone dings in my pocket and I pull it out, reading the text from my brother that he's ready to meet. "Sorry, man. I gotta go. We'll catch up soon. Just let me know if you need anything."

Henry shakes my hand. "Thank you for being my best man. It'll make Kiki happy."

Near the altar, I get a glimpse of Kiki trying to stop Ace from humping his new bride. "It's all about making the bride happy on her big day."

Time to forget that kiss. Like I said, I'm only here to save the brewery and then get my ass back to Atlanta.

SIX

Kiki

NEVER TRUST A FEELING...

SILENCE IS NOT ALWAYS a good thing. It's eerily quiet in my office after the wedding ends and the guests have gone home. Everything has been packed away and now I'm going over the end-of-day reports on the computer.

And it's too damn quiet. That means my thoughts are too damn loud. My face is hot, because what are the odds Ellis is Henry's friend? How did this happen?

"Woohoo," Lola says, entering with a champagne bottle and three plastic glasses. "Congratulations on your first successful wedding."

She pours the bubbly as Poppi walks in and perches on my desk. "Who was that guy Henry had with him?" she asks.

"Nobody," I grunt out. "I mean, his name is Ellis."

"Doesn't sound like nobody." They sip their champagne, eyeing me over the rim.

I take in a deep breath. "Fine, he's Henry's best man." I drain what's in my glass. "And he's kind of the same man who kissed me in the parking lot."

"Trellis guy?" Lola asks, completely surprised. "Ellis is the trellis guy?"

"Oh my god," Poppi joins in. "Ellis the trellis guy. Trellis Ellis."

Ugh. "Yeah."

I push back from my desk, and move my head from side to side, cracking my neck and trying my best to loosen these tense muscles.

"What are you going to do?" Lola asks.

"What do you mean? I'm going to do nothing and pretend it never happened."

"Damn, and I was going to ask you if he was single." Lola fake frowns.

"Well, what do you mean *was*? You can date him. I don't care." Think they believe me?

"I'm not dating him after you've had your lips all over him."

"I haven't had my lips *all* over him." I think back to our kiss. "Just slightly on him."

"You totally have a crush on him, don't you?" Poppi's face dares me to deny it.

"I do not." I cross my arms. "I'm getting married to Henry, remember? And he's perfect for me." He really is. I'm trying to remember all the ways he's just so perfect for me, but I can't think of any right now. These girls have me all flustered. I turn away from them and shut down the computer.

My mind is scrambled like eggs, unable to even hold a thought together.

"So you wouldn't mind if Lola dated him?" Poppi challenges.

I don't dare look at them. "Nope, not at all."

NEVER KISS A STRANGER

"No, it's ok," Lola says. "I was only teasing."

Honestly, I'm kind of wondering if Ellis is single too. Damn traitorous mind. I hate that I'm wondering about this.

Poppi gathers our glasses and throws them in the trash. "You better get moving if you're going to meet Henry for dinner," she says.

"Henry?" I ask, absentmindedly. "Oh, right. Henry." My fiancé. We have plans at an Italian restaurant, because spaghetti is my favorite. I remember when he and I made the plans, I suggested a new little Thai place, but Henry said Italian is always the best selection.

Now that I think of it, I compromised and said we could try Thai next time. I'm always compromising. We gather our things and I can barely focus on my friends chatter as I lock up.

Wonder if Henry will bring Ellis? No, stop that right now, Kiki. No more of this. I need to tell Henry the kiss bandit was his friend.

My mind keeps replaying how Ellis' eyes appeared sad when he found out I was Henry's fiancée. I hate to admit it, but I was a little sad to have him find out too.

"Any word from the farmer, yet?" Lola asks, on our way out, reminding me I'm still waiting on a goat to poop out my ring.

"Nothing yet. I guess my ring made him constipated."

"I'm sure he'll poop soon," the always optimistic Lola singsongs.

"If he doesn't, does that mean the wedding is off?" Poppi asks.

We laugh, but as I drive away, a minuscule part of me finds myself hoping Peter won't poop it out.

———

ELLIS ISN'T with Henry when I arrive at the restaurant and I can't believe there's a small ounce of disappointment settled in the pit of my stomach. I shrug it off as I pass by the candlelit tables covered with checkered tablecloths.

My resolve strengthens to tell Henry as we weave between the diners. I can't go into a marriage full of lies.

Henry stands and kisses my cheek. Why does he never kiss my lips? He goes to pull out the chair for me but then stops when he's distracted by a chime from his phone. He sits. "Did everyone enjoy the dog thing?" he asks, tapping away to whoever sent the message.

I pull out my own chair. "They did." Henry glances up and smiles. "Listen, there's something we need to talk about."

He's back to his phone and I try to think of the best way to tell him about Ellis and me.

"I think you should know that, well, it wasn't my fault." Ugh, I'm botching this and Henry still hasn't even looked up from his phone. We can come back to this topic.

"Sorry." He sets the phone down. "Did everyone enjoy the wedding?"

My stomach twists tighter than the garlic knot in the bread basket.

"They did," I repeat. "I actually just said that. Listen, we need to…" my words fade away as Henry answers a call. He holds his finger up, and then rises and steps away from the table.

With a sigh, I pick up a buttery garlic knot and stuff a large chunk in my mouth. As I chew, I glance around at all the other couples. Most of the men here are in suits, like Henry, and are all more occupied with their phones than the person with them.

The women all look like me, trying to make small talk with a man who can't disconnect from the lifeline in their hand.

Henry returns, and I just don't have it in me anymore to tell him about the kiss. It was one senseless kiss that wasn't my fault, and if Ellis tells him, so be it.

"Sorry," Henry says. "Just need to take care of one more thing."

I give him a tight smile, not that he'd notice since I'm not a phone, and debate the best way to ask him a few things about Ellis.

There's a million questions circulating in my head. Like for starters, who the heck is he? And how does Henry know him?

And I do need to find out if he's single...for Lola, of course. Maybe he's mentioned him all the times I've drowned out his work stories. Ok, from here on out, I promise never to drown out anything Henry ever says again.

But, it's no use because Henry put his phone down and is now saying something to me, and I have no idea what it is.

Whatever he said, he finds my smile and nod acceptable. I probably just agreed to have spaghetti every day for the rest of our lives. Pull it together, Kiki.

Henry picks up the leatherbound menu and studies it. "What are you going to have?"

I can't even think about food right now, but I open my own and skim the entrees, waiting for an item to pop out at me. "Panzanella, maybe."

"But spaghetti is your favorite," he says, his voice raising an octave.

"Well, don't want to over do it," I throw back with a smile.

"Ok, I'm getting the chicken piccata."

The waiter arrives to take our order and when he's gone, now is my chance to ask about his friend while Henry is electronic free.

"So, that man, Ellis, how do you know him?" I ask in a very blasé way. Or at least what I hope is blasé.

"Old friends from high school." He shakes his head with a smile as if he's remembering the good old days. "He moved away right after graduation."

"Why?"

Henry shrugs. "Business. He lives in Atlanta and is only here for a little bit."

I shake off the momentary—inappropriate—sadness and remind myself I'm getting married to this man before me. "So, is he single?" My heart flutters inside my chest. That was so hard to ask, even though I know I'm asking for Lola. "Lola had her eye on him." Come on, I know she didn't. But, that was such a hard question to ask.

"I don't really know, but I'm thinking yes." Henry appears like he's on board for Lola and Ellis dating. I wish I could be right there along with him, but for some reason something is holding me back. "We can have a double date," Henry says.

I need to think of ways *not* to be around Ellis, not for more ways *to* be around him. As soon as the food arrives, I launch into the story about how happy Darlene was with Georgia's wedding, but most of the conversation falls on deaf ears. Henry is back to tapping away on his phone, and is only half-listening to me again.

As soon as dinner is over, Henry leads me out of the restaurant with his arm around my shoulders. "It's still early, why don't we see what Ellis and Lola are up to now?"

Every part of me wants to just go home and call it a day, but I send a text to Lola, and of course, she's up for going out.

After a few minutes, it's settled—we're all hanging out at a tiki bar on the water.

Henry holds my hand as we make our way the few blocks to the beach and toward the neon sign of *Rum Forest Rum*. Inside, we squeeze through the people to the back patio where we find a table, surrounded by tiki torches, and wait for Lola and Ellis to arrive. Henry orders our drinks and when my daiquiri arrives, I suck down a healthy portion. Worse comes to worst, I'll grab a torch and tell Ellis he's voted off the island.

My drink is history by the time I spot Lola in an aquamarine sundress, waving and approaching our table.

"I'm so happy you called," Lola says, smiling.

Before she can sit, I pull her away from Henry, who is focused on the big screen TV.

"It's a set up," I whisper.

Her blue eyes focus on me. "What do you mean? Set up how?"

Before I can get anymore into telling her it was all Henry's idea, Ellis strides into the bar, looking like candy on a stick.

And by the way the women stare at him, they definitely want a lick.

Henry waves him over. It's all happening so fast, and Lola's eyes grow bigger as she connects the dots. I can see it all over her face. And she's not too happy. I mean, sure, she's happy to be hanging out, but she's not on board with this plan.

"I'm not into Ellis," she whispers in my ear as soon as all the hellos have taken place and drinks are flowing.

"Really?" I question her absurdity. In his dark jeans, and simple black t-shirt hugging his biceps, Ellis is the epitome of sexy. If you're into that kind of thing. Which I'm not. I prefer Henry. I mentally slap myself for that thought.

Henry and Ellis chat, while Lola and I edge away from them. "I'm sorry. I panicked, ok?" I tell her.

"Panicked how?"

"I was asking questions about him at dinner, and well, Henry suggested a double date. And I…"

"You were trying to cover up." She points the little black stirrer from her drink at me. "You've got it bad."

"Do not." My cheeks heat. "I really don't."

Ellis and Henry close in on us, and I try to look anywhere but at Ellis.

Finally, I glance up, sneaking a peek at him, and he's laughing at Henry calling him a player.

He hasn't acted in any way for me to suspect he's a player. Normally, you can spot those types of guys immediately. They usually check out every woman in a bar.

But, Ellis hasn't even glanced around. His attention has remained…well, on me. Henry, on the other hand, is acting like a spectator at a museum. He can't stop his eyes from wandering all over the place. Hm. I'm sure he's just getting a feel for his environment. Maybe. I slurp down the rest of my second frozen drink and immediately regret it.

"Brain freeze," I say, pressing a finger to my temple.

Henry wraps an arm around me, kissing my forehead. "Isn't she just adorable?" he says to Ellis.

Ellis has a beer halfway to his mouth and his green eyes sear into me, melting my brain freeze. "Yeah, she is," he drawls out, slowly. "Press your tongue to the roof of your mouth."

Like some voodoo priest, he has now inserted thoughts of his kiss into my brain.

"Let's dance," Lola interrupts our moment, saving me from his hot stare. She grabs my hand and together we mingle into the crowd on the outskirts of the dance floor.

I close my eyes, letting the music distract me.

"He can't stop watching you," Lola says into my ear.

My eyes pop open and find Ellis' in an instant. I turn, so I won't be forced to look at him as I sway my hips. "I need to tell Henry to find another best man."

Lola laughs. "You can't do that."

"Yes, I can."

"You're just gonna have to suck it up and deal with him."

"He lives in Atlanta. He's not in town for very long."

Lola shakes her body to the beat. "See, you'll be fine. Just don't be alone with him. Ever."

I stop dancing. "I can be alone with him. I'm not that crazy that I can't even be alone with the man."

"Well, better not to chance it."

"He's Henry's friend. Nothing's going to happen between us." And I hope I'm right. Because my mind is all over the place.

I love Henry, don't I?

The engagement happened so fast, and I don't think I ever took the time to process exactly what being married actually means.

But, I do love him. Don't I?

He's very...work oriented. That's a great quality. And he doesn't just randomly kiss people in parking lots making them blush. But he also doesn't make me feel hot like Ellis is right now. It's like scorching hot. I've heard about someone lighting you on fire, but damn. Feels like my skin is melting. This is so bad.

Before I can process what this heat means, he's stalking toward me as Henry chats up the waitress next to them. Actually, it's more of a run. And then, I'm swept into his arms.

"Fuck," he says. "You're on fire."

He doesn't mean figuratively. I'm literally on fire. They should have a warning sign by the tiki torches for buzzed people like me.

Lola gasps and tosses her drink on my skirt just before Ellis' hands fondle my thighs putting out the small flame but creating a raging wildfire within me. I've really got to stop with these cliché comparisons.

His warm fingers graze against my skin, leaving a trail of goosebumps. "You're ok," he assures me, rising from his crouched position. "Just a little charred."

He steps back and grazes his teeth over his bottom lip before abruptly turning and crossing to Henry who is oblivious to the fact his fiancée was nearly just roasted.

As I watch Ellis walk away, I realize I'm not ok at all.

SEVEN

Ellis

NEVER TRUST A FLAME...

I SHOULD LEAVE. Seriously. I should. When Henry texted me earlier about meeting up, I didn't think that meant with him and...*her*.

The same her I can't stop thinking about.

But, I need to. Because she's the most off-limits person in the universe for me right now. It's obvious tonight's a set-up with her blonde friend.

And Lola seems nice. But, there's just something about Kiki. I can't quite put my finger on it.

"Thanks for coming out tonight, man," Henry says, clapping his hand on my shoulder. "And for saving my bride-to-be."

I smile. "Don't mention it." I feel like telling him next time maybe a head's up if he plans on bringing the fiancée.

But, I don't want to be one of *those* guys. I need to squash whatever feeling this is I'm having for Kiki into the ground. And get my head in the game.

"Kiki's great," he nods in her direction, "but she has me doing all this wedding stuff that I just don't have time for."

"Like what?"

Henry leans closer. "Flowers and cake and shit. She wants me involved every step of the way."

"And you don't want to be?" I ask.

"It's not that. I just don't have time. I'm going for partner at the investment firm I work for. They're looking for a very specific type of candidate. They want a married, dedicated, solid man. Team player...you know what I mean, right?"

"Yeah, I get it." My eyes travel to Kiki on the dancefloor and I feel odd about watching her shake her ass with Henry standing right next to me. "Speaking of...I was wondering if your firm would be interested in helping out our brewery."

Henry's eyes light up. "Absolutely. You help me out with wedding bullshit, I'll help you out by investing."

Just what I wanted to hear. And besides, I need to find a reason *not* to like Kiki. Maybe if I spend more time with her I'll see how perfect she is for Henry, and I'll be able to stop with this little fantasy obsession I have about her. "Perfect, then I'm your man," I hear myself say before I've fully thought it through.

Henry's eyes light up. "Really? I love this." He shakes my hand.

I shrug. "Why not, I've got a little time on my hands." The brewery is top priority, so what's a few hours here and there so I can get this Kiki out of my mind and possibly garner points with Henry to put The Bearded Goat into the 'exclusive' category.

Henry pats me on the back. "I really appreciate it." He nods toward the girls. "That Lola is pretty, huh?"

I take a swig of my beer. "Sure." I couldn't even tell you

Lola's eye color. But I can tell you how Kiki's are the color of caramel with golden flecks around the iris. Ridiculous, I know.

The girls stop dancing and rejoin us. Henry kisses Kiki on the cheek. It's a little odd to me that they aren't a touchy-feely kind of couple. My mind suddenly transports to the other day when my lips were on hers. I set my beer down. "I'll be back." I have to get away from her for a minute.

I head off in search of the restroom, so I can clear my head.

Before I can even make it to the back of the place, there's a tap on my shoulder. I spin around and am met by those hypnotizing eyes of Kiki's.

Does she even know how pretty her eyes are?

"Henry just told me you'll be helping me pick out flowers. I just wanted to let you know that I don't need your help."

I cross my arms. "That so?"

"Yes." She nods. "Furthermore, I don't think you and I should be hanging around one another."

"I disagree." How else am I supposed to woo Henry?

"What?" Her cute little button nose turns up in disgust. "I don't need you."

I step closer, so a man can get by us in the narrow hallway. Kiki's back presses against the wall and her eyes challenge mine. "I think you'll need me." I don't mean to sound so sexual, but my god, she's making this so hard. I mean, difficult.

"You're a flower guru, huh?"

I laugh. "Flower whisperer. Come on. Let me help you."

She purses her lips together. Those same lips I kissed and can't stop thinking about. "Ok, fine. But don't think I'm going to get whatever kind of flowers you pick."

I wink. "We'll see." And I hope she does. I need to get past these feelings of wanting her.

ON MONDAY, I head over to Bearded Goat Brewery, to finally have a face to face with Urban to discuss the possibility of Henry's firm.

Urban looks up from the papers on his desk when I enter his office. "Time to talk, big brother," I say with a grin.

"Ellis, so good to see you, man." He stands and pulls me in for a hug. "I might shed a tear," he jokes.

"Careful, might lose that badass reputation you have," I tease him.

"I'm secure in my manhood," he says, releasing me and resuming his seat.

I'll admit, I've missed my brother.

Normally, I wait until he comes to Atlanta, because I don't come home hardly ever. Not because I dislike it here in Florida, it's actually a great place, but I just don't like dealing with him.

It's one thing to run into family, and then it's a completely other thing to keep running into my father.

I swear the man is unavoidable, and I still can't comprehend how Urban is able to stay here and continue to work for him. I guess I'll never understand it.

Urban's hazel eyes study me as I take a seat in the leather club chair positioned in front of his desk. "Being home is weird, huh?" he asks.

"Just a little." I force a smile.

"Don't worry. He's not here."

"Ah, ok." My body relaxes as I thank my lucky stars the asshole isn't around.

"He doesn't come in much anymore."

I pick up a small silver frame from the cluster on his desk and stare at Urban's wiener. Dog, that is. "He just likes the title still," I surmise.

Urban laughs a bit. "Yeah, I guess." He leans back in his chair and frowns. "It's not good, El."

"What isn't?"

"The business. The brewery. It's going under."

I return the frame with his dog to its place, hoping I misunderstood. "How can that be? Things were going so well."

Urban rakes a hand through his hair, his frown now a permanent feature on his face. He's older than me by a few years, and he's a fucking wiz at business. I don't see how this could be happening with him running the operation. Unless...

"Is it because of *him*?"

"Yeah." He worries the corner of his lip and then continues, "He's developed a bit of a gambling addiction."

"Of course, he has," I mutter.

Urban stares at my throat, not meeting my eyes. "I've been having to bail him out with a lot of the profits."

I stand and cross to the window, looking at the rows of cars in the employee lot. Lots of people depend on a paycheck from this business. "Dammit, Urban. What about the IRS?"

"We're fine there, promise. He took it out as a loan from the company."

"Let me guess, he's gonna default on the loan?" I shake my head. "How long have we got until we're completely fucked?"

Urban scrubs a hand across the stubble on his jaw. "We'll be completely out of business within the year."

"No fucking way." I had no idea it was this bad. Guilt slams into me like a concrete wall. I should have been here.

"I'm sorry. It all happened rather suddenly." He pushes back his chair and stands. "The market is oversaturated, Ellis." Urban walks around his desk, leaning back against it, slipping his hands into the pockets of his khakis. He doesn't say anything, just stares at me for a moment. "I don't know if anything will help at this point. It would be like throwing a water bottle at a blazing fire."

I pinch the bridge of my nose. Giving up is not an option. "Remember Henry Faniki?" I ask.

He smiles for the first time since he started telling me about the business. "Yeah, how is he? I haven't seen him in ages. Isn't he in real estate?"

"Investment firm. He's doing great. I ran into him here at the pub." I tell him about our conversation and my plan to get the brewery on his firm's radar with a push from Henry. "He's getting married and he asked me to be his best man. So, I said yes."

"Really?" Urban stares at me for a moment. "Wasn't he always going from girl to girl?"

"Yeah," I answer. "Sort of like you."

"Can't help it if I haven't met the one," he says with a wink. "When's the big day?"

"A few weeks. I'm not really sure." My face grows serious. "I asked him about investing in the brewery."

"Ah, what did he say?"

"Said I help him, he'll help me."

Urban smiles. "Perfect, you better be the best damn best man he's ever seen." He laughs.

I don't laugh along, wondering if I should fill my brother in on the rest of the story. "I met his fiancée."

"Is she nice?"

"Yeah, seems to be."

His eyes narrow. "What aren't you telling me?"

"Well…" I pause but know he will keep on till I come clean, "we kind of kissed."

Urban raises both brows. "Kind of? What do you mean? Like a long time ago?"

"No. Right after I got into town." He lets out a low whistle. "It was stupid. I'd broken this trellis thing in the parking lot, and she was yelling at me, and Dad and Yasmin were driving by. And I just knew if they saw me they'd stop, and I just couldn't face him, yet. So, I did the first thing I could think of and grabbed her."

"And you kissed her? Did she slap you?"

I laugh, remembering back to Kiki's reaction of our kiss. "She was pretty pissed."

"You gonna tell Henry?"

I pace the large office. "What do you think?"

"Was it just a kiss? Or are you wanting more?"

My brother knows me so well. It's been ages since we've had a real talk about feelings and women. Normally, we talk shop or about the latest sports game and head on our way.

"I'll be fine."

He smiles. "I didn't ask that, Ellis. You have a thing for this girl?"

My face grows hot with his line of questioning. Under different circumstances, I would have already asked this girl out to dinner. I'd already be planning my second date with her, and how I could get to kissing her again. Full time. But, this is not *that* circumstance. "If things were different, sure. But, they're not."

"So, what are you going to do?"

"Well, I'm gonna be his best man, save this company, and head back to Atlanta. Why?"

Urban laughs, a long hearty laugh. "It all sounds so easy."

"It will be. We just need some options. Some fresh new ideas."

"Options meaning different women?"

Now it's my turn to laugh. "Always thinking with your dick. Different *business* options. Products. Anything. Something we can bring to Henry's firm."

"Yes, brilliant idea." Urban sits back behind his desk, bringing his computer to life. "Let me go over some of the numbers with you."

"Does Dad know I'm here?" I move around to stand behind Urban, so I can see the computer screen.

"Yeah, I told him you were coming into town."

"What does he say about the brewery?"

"He doesn't know."

Asshole. I doubt he would even care. "I'm sure he's busy with other things. Do you see him a lot?"

He nods. "Brunch every Sunday with him and Yasmin at the club."

"Ah, the club." Pretentious motherfuckers. I hate that life. I hate the life my father represents.

And the life he's tried to push onto his kids.

"I could really use your help while you're in town. I don't need the stress of you and Dad fighting."

"Yeah, man," I assure him. "I'm here to help. I don't even want to see him."

"You know you can stay with me. I have more than enough room."

"Nah, it's ok. I don't mind the hotel."

"Well, the offer is there."

Urban moves the mouse around, clicking on a file on the desktop screen, and my phone pings in my pocket. I glance at a text from Kiki with the name of the flower shop she wants to meet at next week.

"Henry?" Urban asks.

"The girl."

He shakes his head as he pulls up the financials. "You're worse off than I thought."

I'm in deep. "Henry asked so I'm just helping her with a few things for the wedding."

"Is that such a good idea?"

I nod. "I'm sure after spending a few hours with her, I'll realize her and Henry are perfect for each other and I'll not want her anymore."

Urban shakes his head. "Sounds like a solid plan, buddy."

"Don't patronize me. What other choice do I have?"

"You could bow out of this wedding."

"Nah, I'll be fine. Besides, we need the investment. Don't worry, I'm a big boy."

He laughs. "Sure, you are. Now let me show you last quarter."

We go over the numbers for a bit, and I realize Urban was

right. This is way worse than either of us could have ever thought.

My father has been using the company money like his very own personal piggy bank. The books are a mess, and we'll need an act of God to dig ourselves out of this. But, it's not undoable.

In fact, it's really fucking doable.

EIGHT

Kiki

NEVER TRUST a ghost in a flower shop...

"MARSHA IS GOING to wrap the palm trees with white roses. Isn't that clever? Are you still wanting those wildflowers?"

At this point, maybe my mother should just go to Marsha's wedding instead of my own. I kid. Maybe. Before I enter the flower shop to meet Ellis, I steel myself to not be affected by his presence. All week long, he's been texting me about flowers. Which then turned into an exchange of wedding planning memes. Which then led me to realize, Henry and I do not have the same sense of humor. When I showed him one of the memes, he said, "Huh, I don't get it. What's so funny about that?"

Humor is so important. When times are tough, I need someone who can make me laugh. Ellis thought it was hilarious.

But he's not going to be my husband. He's not my anything and this is why I need to nip this in the bud. Pardon the pun.

When I step inside the fragranced store, he stands near a display of roses, outshining their beauty.

"Hi," I greet him.

He's not as attractive as I initially thought. Seriously, he's not. Ok, I'm a huge liar. The man is gorgeous. And I don't know why I even agreed to let him help me, but honestly...I need the help.

Henry doesn't want to be involved with the planning, which I understand. I get it. I do. He's got a lot going on with work and trying to become a partner. But, I wish I wasn't so drawn to the man he asked to help me in his place.

Wait. I didn't just think that. I'm not attracted to Ellis. I'm...curious?

Yes, that's what I'm going with. I'm curious about him. Like what's his favorite...everything.

And I know I shouldn't be having any of those types of emotions about my fiancé's best man.

Well, that can change. I'm sure I can find fault in this guy. I mean, look at how he's walking around this flower shop like a fish out of water.

"So, flowers, huh?" He grabs a rose and smiles.

Ugh, there's definitely no fault in him there. His lips have a perfect bow and they're extremely distracting. Ah, yes. That's a fault. Henry's lips aren't distracting. They're a little thin and less come hither, and perfectly safe.

Henry—1

Ellis—0

Against my will, my eyes scan his jeans and black button-down shirt as he picks up a calla lily. He glances at me over the top of the petals, and I should really call Henry.

Maybe if I hear my fiancé's voice it will break the spell and remind me I'm getting married soon.

I pull out my phone but quickly push it back into my bag when the flower shop attendant stalks closer.

"Can I help you?" the raven-haired woman asks.

"Yes, I'm getting married and would like to look at some options you have for the ceremony."

She smiles, glancing between me and Ellis. If she mistakes us for the happy couple like in every romantic comedy movie, I will lose it.

"Sure, I have a binder. Let me find it. I'm Alice, by the way. You two can have a seat at the table out back, and I'll be right there."

"Thank you." Ellis leads the way past a display of begonia plants and opens the door for me. I brush past him, holding my breath so I don't breathe in his intoxicating scent.

We walk toward a wrought-iron table surrounded by a garden of colorful flowers. "This is nice," I tell him.

He shrugs. "I don't really know much about flowers. I'm more of a beer guy."

See. Right there. Another fault. He's an alcoholic who drinks a lot of beer. Although, he doesn't have a beer gut. I glance at his torso that's probably etched with a six-pack. My hand moves closer to his stomach, and then, as if it doesn't belong to me, it runs over his shirt.

"What are you doing?" he asks.

"I can't believe I just did this." I remove my hand as quickly as I can.

Ellis laughs. "What were you looking for there?"

He pulls my chair out for me, shocking me that he's such a gentleman. He probably throws his jacket over puddles too. Based on the fire incident, Henry probably wouldn't notice if I fell in a manhole. But that's ok. I'm a survivor. Yes, letting me rescue myself is good.

Henry—2

Ellis—0

I take a seat, square my shoulders, and let the truth free. "A six-pack."

Ellis' eyes meet mine. "Well, I can assure you it's there."

And it certainly is. He lifts his shirt. Like a peep show just for me. I feel like maybe I should throw a dollar bill at him, but I can't move. Instead, I'm gawking like I've never seen a six-pack up close and personal like this.

And, I realize I never have. Sure, I've seen six-packs in pictures. I've seen the movie *Magic Mike*. I know what they look like. But, I've never seen one out in the wild like this. Even his belly button is perfect.

I mean, I love Henry, I do, but he does *not* have chiseled abs like Ellis. Or that carved vee. And that's fine with me. Because Ellis would probably expect me to have one too. And the only six-pack I have is sparkling cranberry juice in my fridge.

Henry—3

Ellis—0

Ellis drops his shirt and takes a seat next to me. "If you want to keep staring at it, I'll have to charge you."

I laugh, a bit too much, and quickly stop. "No, I mean, no. I didn't even enjoy that."

Ellis smiles. "You're a very strange cookie, Kiki."

Before I can respond, Alice approaches with two thick black binders nearly falling out of her thin arms. Ellis hops up, meeting her half-way and quickly taking the binders from her. See, he has a hero complex. And if I'm being honest, it's...endearing.

As a woman, I'm perfectly capable of taking care of myself. I do it every day. But the cave woman in me can't help appreciating a man who is protective. Alice agrees with my traitorous thoughts, judging by the size of her smile.

She leaves us to browse the voluminous selection, and I fixate on flipping through the binder for the second perfect flowers for the wedding, since forget-me-nots are out of the equation. There's an oppressive silence, as I turn the pages of one binder and Ellis the other. To his credit, he really looks interested in what's on the page. Like he might care about what flower we have.

"Why did you kiss me?" I blurt out.

His head moves slowly to me. "I...uhh." He snaps his binder closed and turns in his seat a little to face me. "My father was driving by, and I didn't want him to see me. I'm so sorry. Had I known you were engaged I would have never—"

"I know," I cut him off. "I'm sorry."

He places his hand over mine, and a zing travels up my arm. "No, you have nothing to be sorry about. I'm the idiot who kissed a friend's fiancée. You didn't have on a ring."

"My ring was swallowed by a goat."

Ellis laughs—it's mesmerizing—and I laugh a little too, hoping mine is as good as his. "I'm still waiting on the farm to call."

"I was not expecting you to say that." He leans in and his eyes drop to my mouth. "What did Henry say about it?"

"Nothing, actually." His closeness makes me want to withdraw, but I don't. He smells divine. It's not an overpowering expensive cologne you can't get away from like Henry wears. His scent is clean and understated, making you want to seek it out. "I didn't elaborate."

He tilts his head, puzzled for a moment. "He didn't want the details of that story? I know I do."

I shrug. Now I'm wondering why Henry *didn't* press me for details? It's not every day a goat eats your ring. I'm also wondering why I find myself telling Ellis every detail of the story and enjoying the amused expression on his face.

"That's the best thing ever," he says when I'm finished relaying what happened. "So, wait. How do you get it back?"

"Well, eventually the goat will..."

"Stop." He places a finger on my suddenly dry lips. "I think I get it, and I don't know if I can handle it."

I giggle behind his finger. And then, my laughter fades when he traces his finger tip over my mouth. His eyes are so intense, I inadvertently lick my lips, grazing his finger. His jaw clenches as he pulls his hand back.

"I'm sorry. I shouldn't have done that."

"Why did you?" I ask.

"The flowers told me to."

I straighten up in my chair. "Ah. Haunted flowers?"

Ellis smiles. "Yeah." He taps the binder. "These flowers are all haunted, and you shouldn't have any of them at your wedding."

"Well, that's more for Marsha," I say, without thinking.

"Who's Marsha?"

"My cousin. She's getting married too." I look down at the binder and trail my finger along the edge. "My mom is in psychological warfare with my Aunt over which daughter has the best life. I'm losing."

"Ah," he says as if he has completely grasped the entirety of the situation from that one sentence. "I find it hard to believe that Marsha could beat you in anything." His eyes sweep over my face. "Don't try to win someone else's race."

This is getting very deep, and I'm sorry but…

Henry—3

Ellis—I can't quantify it.

"We can't kiss again, Ellis." I get my serious face on, like when I'm reprimanding one of the puppies for pooping on the floor. "I'm getting married." My voice is so low and serious, I almost don't like the sound of it. But this has to stop.

"I'm sorry. Won't happen again. I should go." He stands, and for a split second, I want to tell him not to leave. But, I don't. I only watch as he walks back in the store. Sometimes, the right thing is the hardest to do.

I flip the pages in the binder, but as hard as I try, I can't focus on the flowers.

"Sorry, it took me so long," Alice says, bustling out the door and toward me with a smile. "Your friend said to give you this because he thinks it'll be the perfect flower for your wedding."

She lays a bunch of blue forget-me-nots on the table. Of all the flowers, he chose this one. What are the odds? An ache settles in my chest as I touch the soft, blue petals. I'm not sure I can forget Ellis, no matter how much I try.

⊏▭⊐

TODAY, I finally got the call. Yes, *the* call. The goat has finally produced something for me. When I shoot a text to Poppi and tell her I'm on my way out to the farm, she offers to come along. I should be excited, but for some reason I'm not. Those flowers really were haunted. And now I am. Haunted by Ellis. He's creeping around my mind, with his abs and forget-me-nots, and honestly, it's starting to scare me.

"Thanks for coming," I tell Poppi when she picks me up at my house. Yes, I asked her to drive.

Her blue Subaru is better than my big ol' work van, but the real reason I wanted her to drive is I'm working on exorcising Ellis. The van and the trellis will only make me think of him more.

"Lola says you all went out last night." She plugs in the address to the farm into her GPS and turns on the radio.

"Yeah, Henry wanted to set up his friend, Ellis, with Lola."

I can see the skepticism on her face. "Really? How did that work out?"

I fiddle with the seatbelt. "Well, I'm sure he liked Lola."

She stops at a red light and faces me. "Are you disappointed?"

"No," I lie. "I saw him a few days ago to pick out flowers."

She tucks a long red wave behind her ear. "Kiki, what are you doing? Maybe you're not ready to get married."

I stare out the window, watching the trees pass in a blur.

"No, I am. I really am." I think. Or am I inadvertently running a race for my mom?

"It all happened so fast. Maybe you and Henry need a longer engagement. Like, what's the rush?"

"I'm not really sure."

"Do you love him?" She makes a left off the main road and onto a gravel road flanked by open grass. She parks her car near the entrance of the farm. "Like really love him?"

"Of course, I do." I think. I'm not so sure anymore.

We exit the car and walk toward an open metal gate with wood-carved animals on each side.

"Wow, this is beautiful," Poppi says as we cross through the gate and into what feels like a different world.

A mottled gray farmhouse sits quietly on a luxurious green field, dotted with cows and horses, and off to the left is a big red barn. It's your typical farm everyone has read about growing up in storybooks. I'm more of a city girl, but I can tell Poppi is falling in love with the beauty surrounding us by the minute.

And now I'm not sure if it's the farm she loves, or the rugged cowboy headed our way. He steps closer, his eyes twinkling in the soft sunlight dancing through the leaves of the trees.

"Howdy there." He smiles, taking off his cowboy hat. "I'm Gavin. You must be here for the ring."

"Hi," Poppi says, "yes we are."

"I'm glad Peter was a good boy," I tell him.

Gavin laughs. "Yeah, that little bugger took forever to produce that ring." He holds it out.

I reach for it, and then retract my hand. The thought of Peter pooping out my ring and what exactly that means never really crossed my mind.

"Um, we disinfected and sanitized it really well for you."

"Uh, thanks." I stare at the ring and then take it from Gavin's outstretched hand. I slip it on my finger and gaze at the way the diamond reflects from the sun. My finger feels like it's choking for air.

"Want a quick tour?" Gavin asks us.

"Yes, sure," Poppi says and then introduces herself and me to him. She whispers to me as we follow him toward a fenced in grassy area, "I think I'm in love."

He stops outside a goat pen entrance, and I spot Peter immediately on top of a climbing contraption.

As I watch Peter bounce around with his adorable friends, I immediately picture Henry. I swear, if Henry were a goat, he'd look like Peter. They're like twins separated at birth. Is that bad?

Poppy and Gavin chat about farm things and I rest my arms on the weathered wood, watching the baby goats climb and play. I try to gauge if one looks like anyone else I know—preferably Ellis.

Gavin and Poppi walk off toward a section with chickens, and he calls for me to join them.

"I love animals," Poppi says, dropping a few seeds for some of the smaller chickens.

"I love animals too," Gavin says, looking into Poppi's eyes. "Obviously. Hence the farm."

It feels a bit like I'm watching a mating ritual. I'm waiting for him to throw off his hat, lasso and mount her. I'm so close to asking for his number for her, but then I realize things shouldn't be rushed. So, I hang back, feeding the chickens and glancing at my engagement ring that now feels a bit too heavy for my hand.

Maybe Poppi is right. Maybe everything is moving all too fast. Maybe Henry and I should wait. I mean, why are we rushing?

When he asked me, I was so happy. But, I think it was more the thrill of planning the wedding, having the husband, having it all—having my mother's excitement. Now that I really think about it, everything is moving at supersonic speeds.

I'm so confused, and I glance over at Gavin and Poppi as they make googly eyes at each other and think back if Henry and I looked at each other like that. Have we? I just don't know.

I can't even remember anything right now.

It's that Ellis. He's gone and messed everything all up. I can't think straight whenever he's around. Even when he's not around.

I'm haunted.

I mosey back over to the baby goats. Wonder if Peter has a little girlfriend he wants to marry? Would baby goat weddings ever be a thing?

I snap a picture of Peter as he shows me his teeth. I swear I think he remembers me.

Ellis probably would've gotten a kick out of coming here today. If I had to guess, I think he likes animals. He was digging Georgia's wedding. Unlike Henry who thought it was all one big joke.

"There you are," Poppi says, walking over to stand next to me. "Gavin asked me to dinner."

I raise an eyebrow. "Really?"

Poppi glances over her shoulder to make sure we're alone. "He sounds perfect. He opened this farm with his father and they've rescued over a hundred and fifty animals."

"That's incredible."

"I was thinking we could somehow team up with their farm and Dog Spaw." Poppi's eyes glow with admiration. "I think we could do great things together."

I laugh a little. "I'm sure you'd like to do some great things with him."

She smiles. "Shut up. That's not what I meant." She nudges her elbow into my arm. "But that too."

Gavin makes his way back over to us, and before we go, he says, "I'm really sorry about the goat eating your ring, but it was nice meeting the both of you." He lets go of my hand and shakes Poppi's. "It was really nice meeting you, Poppi. I'll call you."

She smiles. "I hope you do."

We leave Gavin behind, and on the drive home, Poppi says,

"As your best friend, there's a little something I need to get off my chest."

I turn to face her. "Ok."

"I kind of think you're moving too fast with Henry. There, I said it. I would regret it, if I didn't say anything." She glances over at me. "I just want you to be happy, Kiki. And if you really believe Henry can make you that way, then I'll back off."

I chew on the inside of my mouth. "I think he can." But, do I? Do I really think Henry can make me happy? Do I make him happy?

"Just think about it."

"I will, promise."

Little does she know, that's all I've been thinking about.

NINE

Ellis

NEVER DINE WITH THE ENEMY...

"YOU BETTER BE THERE ON TIME," I text Urban.

Realistically, I know I can't avoid my father the whole time I'm here—even if that's exactly what I planned—so when Urban invited me to dinner with both Dad and Yasmin, I agreed. Every part of me would rather pick lint off the floor of my hotel carpet, but I still dress in the suit I brought along and head out for a dreaded family gathering.

On the drive to the country club, Urban doesn't respond, and I'm tempted to cancel.

Sometimes you have to man up, so I turn the rental I'm driving into the parking lot of the Ocean Reef Club and head toward the valet. As he drives away, I kind of want to chase him down and say never mind. Got to man up, though. Before I enter the building, I send Urban another text.

"Fancy seeing you here," a male voice says behind me.

I pocket my phone and turn to see Henry. "Hey. What are you doing here?"

"Taking Kiki out to eat," he says as we step through the glass doors. "We were supposed to meet my parents, but they backed out. What about you?"

I deflate instantly at the mention of his fiancée. "Same, dinner with my father and brother."

The very second I mention my father, he materializes out of thin air, standing next to Henry. "Henry Faniki, it's been so long." My father shakes Henry's hand and his smooth demeanor and ramrod straight back piss me off. I don't know what it is about the man, but even the way he breathes pisses me off.

Maybe because I wish he wasn't.

Yes, I should be punished for the way I'm thinking right now. And as if by magic, the woman I'd love to do the punishing walks toward us in a tight black dress that shows lots of delectable legs. Her hair is swept back off her neck in a low ponytail, and I stare a second too long at the exposed skin. What would it be like to touch her there? God, she's stunning.

"Ellis, hi." Her brow furrows but she recovers smoothly with a smile. "I don't believe we've met," she says to my father. "I'm Kiki, Henry's fiancée."

While my father gushes over their marriage, Urban and Yasmin appear.

"Please have dinner with us," I hear my father say. Before I can interject about how bad of an idea it is, we're entering the dining area and tables are being pushed together for the six of us. I should have stayed in my hotel and counted the lint.

"A bottle of red and a bottle of white for the table," my father tells the waiter, like he has all the money in the world. He doesn't.

And I have no luck. Somehow, I end up seated between Kiki and my brother. It's ok. I'll just keep to myself and let my inner monologue entertain me.

"So, she's the one?" Urban leans over and whispers in my ear.

"She's not *the* one. But, yes, she's *that* one." The minute I turn away from my brother, Kiki's leg brushes against mine under the table. My dick twitches from the contact.

This is too much. I can't deal with this. Why am I so attracted to her? Why does every little thing she does turn me on? It's not like I can't find someone who isn't fucking off limits.

"So, tonight's a special night. My son is back in town, and we're going to celebrate Henry getting married to this lovely woman beside him," my father, obviously a tad bit drunk already, says as the waiter returns and fills wine glasses.

I smile a polite, tight smile and raise my glass. "Glad to be home."

Yasmin decides to input her two cents, "We're so happy you're here, Ellis." She assembles her collagen-filled lips into a smile. "Aren't we, Richard?"

My father nods, pretending he has the perfect family. I don't know who he's trying to impress. Henry? Kiki? The waiters? I'm sure it's more the other members of the club, but I smile back like I don't wish I had daggers to throw at him.

I don't want to make a scene with Kiki here. A man who throws a temper tantrum in public can't call himself a man. I can act like an adult here.

After we order, I reach for my water glass and bump hands with Kiki reaching for the same glass.

"Your glass is on your right," she says, leaning toward me a little, letting me get a whiff of her sweet perfume.

Her scent transports me back to the afternoon I kissed her. "Right, sorry. Haven't been in a country club in years." I take a gulp of water. "I prefer something with less etiquette."

She smiles. "Yeah. I really only need one fork."

Exactly. This isn't my life. And if I'm being honest, I don't want it to be.

Urban likes this lifestyle. He enjoys brunch on Sundays and

playing golf. Me, I want more than superficial. I want to enjoy myself when I'm with my family, not put on a show for everyone to see.

It makes me wonder about Kiki. Is this the life she wants?

It's obvious Henry fits right into this lifestyle. I bet he even hangs out at this club on weekends.

I'm a silent observer as Yasmin makes small talk with Kiki about her business, while I drain my wine.

"You do dog weddings?" Yasmin asks, lighting up. "I'd love to contact you about that for my babies."

Kiki hands over her contact information, and I silently wish her luck with the spoiled balls of fluff Yasmin totes around in a designer bag.

"Speaking of weddings," Henry says, "you up for eating some cake tomorrow in my place?" He stares right at me, waiting for my response.

"No, no, it's ok," Kiki says. "I can go with Lola or Poppi." The ring on her left finger reflects the light from the chandelier overhead and nearly blinds me. I guess she finally got it back from the goat holding it hostage.

Urban laugh/coughs, and I give him a glare before turning my attention back on Henry. "Sure, I could eat some cake. But only if Kiki wants me to come along."

"You're helping plan the wedding?" my father asks. "Watch yourself," he directs to Kiki. "You'll have a champagne disaster if he's helping you."

I think back to his wedding to Yasmin, and how I tried to ruin the whole thing. I almost did, but in the end, they finally went through with it, and were married. But, like I said, not for lack of trying on my part.

"It was just a few bottles," I tell my father. "Excuse me." I need a break from his phony smile. His phony life.

From his phony everything. Kiki looks at me with questioning eyes as I stand. If circumstances were different, I'd take her with me. I'd grab her hand and we'd run to the back, and I'd sweep her into my arms.

She'd blush as I trace my fingers over her cheek. She'd moan as I lean in to kiss her.

We'd leave from here, never looking back.

But circumstances aren't different, so I weave between the tables toward the back of the restaurant in search of somewhere to escape. I find something—a little hidden patio off the back.

I step outside and breathe in the balmy night air. The ocean is close, I can smell the salty sea, and some of the stress leaves my shoulders.

"That's some major tension at that table," Kiki says, joining me on the patio, overlooking the golf course.

"My father and I don't really get along."

She smiles. "Really? I hadn't noticed," she says with playful sarcasm in her tone. "Why not?"

I perch on the half wall enclosing the patio. "It's a long story."

She scoots a little closer. God, she's beautiful with the moonlight dancing across her skin. "I kind of like long stories. I mean, it must be some major emotional baggage to kiss a stranger, just so you don't have to see him."

I stuff my hands in my pockets, so I don't grab her and kiss her again. "Sorry about that." But, am I really sorry? Every part of me knows it was so wrong, yet, I don't regret it.

Although, I should. And that's the most fucked up part.

"I see you got the ring back." I nod toward her left hand, changing the subject.

She lifts her hand, staring at the ring on her finger. "Yeah." Then, she turns to face me. "Is it bad every time I look at it I think about goat poo?"

I can't help laughing at her words. "That's not a good thing."

She shrugs. "I know."

I gaze into her gorgeous brown eyes, letting the thought of her and Henry marinate for a moment. "What are you doing with a guy like him?" My gut says he just doesn't seem right for her.

She steps back, appearing off balance. "What do you mean? I love him."

I step closer, my heart slamming against my ribcage. "Do you really?" If she tells me she loves him, and I believe her, I'll step away and never question her again.

"Of course, I do. I'm getting married to him. And you're going to be the best man." She pokes a finger in my chest, her eyes wide. "You can't ask me questions like that." She rushes back inside.

Fuck. Why did I cross the line and question her about Henry? I want to go after her and apologize, but I know I can't do that with everyone at the table. I need to get her alone, for like five minutes so I can apologize.

Guess I'll be eating cake tomorrow.

WHO IS the person that decided to have cake at a wedding? I want to personally shake that man or woman's hand. Because cake tasting is fucking incredible.

What's not incredible is the awkwardness that's settled between Kiki and myself as we sample different kinds of cake. She hasn't looked me in the eyes since we got here over twenty minutes ago.

Last night, the rest of dinner I stayed silent, only answering questions when asked. I tried not to rock the boat, as they'd call it. I didn't need Henry and Kiki to know the inner workings of my broken family tree.

Or worse yet, the inner thoughts I've been having about Kiki.

But, that all ends today. I'm here for the cake, nothing else.

74

Swear.

The sales lady drones on and on about the different kinds of cake we're eating, and I kind of wish she'd just go away so I could start my apology.

"And this last one is red velvet, which most don't do for a spring wedding. That's when the two of you are getting married, right? Spring?" The older lady clasps her plump hands together over her heart as she stares at the two of us.

"We're not getting married," Kiki rushes out. "He's the best man."

"Yeah, I'm just helping out."

The woman's head snaps back, like she just made the biggest faux pas in history. "I'm so sorry. But," she smiles at me, "lucky you, right?"

I hold up my fork with the velvet cake on the end of it. "Yep, lucky me."

When she finally walks away, I turn to Kiki. "Listen, I wanted to apologize about last night. I shouldn't have questioned you about Henry."

Kiki sets her fork down. "It's ok. Maybe it is all too soon. I don't know."

I swipe a strand of her brown hair behind her ear. "No, you love him. Don't let me make you think you don't. I was wrong."

So totally fucking wrong.

"But, do I love him?"

God, I want to kiss her again. Is it so wrong that I want to? My heart pounds in frustration at the thought that I can *not* kiss her. Although, I can't remove my hand from her hair. "You do."

"Do I?" Her eyes search mine, as if I'm going to give her the correct answer.

I'm not. I don't even remember what we're talking about. All I can remember is this is so utterly wrong. "Kiki…" I pause, because I should fucking stand up and walk right out of this heavenly little cake shop, but come on, you know I can't do that.

This girl holds some sort of spell over me, making me unable to move. I'm completely frozen.

"What?" she whispers back. Her voice sounds like sex. Like she wants it more than I do, which is physically impossible.

Keep it together, Ellis. Keep your fucking shit together. "Yes, you love him." That was by far one of the hardest things I've ever said to anyone.

She nods her head, and I drop my hand. "Right, of course." But she doesn't look so confident from my words. Hell, even I'm not sure if she loves the guy.

"How long have you two been together?" I ask her, right before taking a bite of the red velvet.

"A little over a month."

I nearly choke on the cake.

I was not expecting that. I figured at least six months.

Although, if I met a girl like Kiki, I'd put a ring on her finger before anyone else could too.

I glance at her diamond, and her eyes follow my path. "I can't stop thinking about poop when I stare at it," she says. I laugh. "I feel like I've washed it so many times. Did I tell you the goat that swallowed it even looked like Henry?"

I laugh again. "He looked like Henry?"

"Yes, I took a picture." She pulls out her phone and taps at the screen and then thrusts it into my face.

A little goat smiles for the camera. "Great picture." I study it, a little closer this time, and fuck, she's right. "He may resemble Henry a little." I can't agree with her and tell her she's marrying a guy who looks like a goat. "But, it isn't an exact replica."

She takes her phone back and plops it into her handbag. "Well, I didn't say he was an exact replica. I, well...never mind."

Oh, I need to know the rest of her sentence. "What?"

She shakes her head, grabbing her fork and piercing the cake with it. "I can't. It's too mean."

She's piqued my interest. "You know I can keep a secret."

Obviously. I've never told anyone I've kissed her. Well, except my brother, but he doesn't count.

"Promise you won't tell Henry?"

I cross my fingers over my chest. "Yes."

"Well, every time I look at Henry…" she sighs, "now, all I see is the goat."

This is bad. This is way worse than what I thought she was going to say. "I'm sure that will go away with time."

"What if it doesn't?"

"It will."

"But, what if it doesn't."

I can't not let her marry Henry because he resembles a goat who ate her ring. Seriously, I can't make this shit up. But, it still doesn't change the fact I can't be the one held responsible for breaking up this wedding. Even if I've tasted the bride's lips and can't forget the sweet flavor.

I need to find some faults in this woman, and right now I can't find a single one. I don't like to say things are perfect, because I feel like that's just asking for something to go wrong, but she makes me almost believe in perfection.

But, I can't think this way. "Kiki, you're getting cold feet. It'll go away. Henry is a person, not a goat." I can't believe I'm actually having this conversation.

"What if it doesn't?"

She looks so distraught, I want to make it all better. "I promise you, baby, it'll go away." And that baby was just a figure of speech.

Her eyes widen. "You shouldn't call me things like that."

"I know." My heart bashes inside my chest, making my breathing erratic. "I know, Kiki."

Silent, we stare at each other. I should look away, but I can't. Her caramel-colored eyes call to me, like a siren calling to a long, lost ship.

And then I do stand. "I forgot, I've got to meet my brother at the brewery."

But, like she doesn't want this moment to end, she stands too. "Brewery?"

"It's my family's brewery. It's not too far from here." And then I say something I'll most likely regret, "Want to come?"

She smiles. "I'd love to."

TEN

Kiki

NEVER WASTE A BEER...

CONFESSION: I'm a beer girl. I'm realizing in the whirlwind romance that took place with Henry, I somehow forgot that. Maybe because the fancy places he frequents would probably frown upon me ordering a beer.

I order the vanilla cake with buttercream frosting before we leave, and then we make our way to the Bearded Goat Brewery a few blocks over. A thought hits me on the way over about Ellis saying he's more of a beer guy. This is what he meant.

"I can't believe you own this," I say, as we enter the iconic brewpub.

"My father started this brewery, and now my brother and I run it."

"That's so interesting. Can I tell you a secret?"

"You don't like beer?" He smiles.

I shake my head. "I don't. I love it. Your I'd Tap That double IPA is my favorite"

He gives me a lop-sided grin and grabs my hand, sliding our palms together. "Let me show you around."

My hand feels tiny in his—and right. I can't tell you how confused I am about everything. The cake tasting made me a million times more confused about my life. I thought I always wanted to get married. And that's still a dream. One day, I do want to be married with some kids and such but being around Ellis makes me think maybe marriage is too big of a step for me. Maybe I should date more people. People like him, preferably. Ugh, I did *not* just think that. But what would a date with him be like?

Is it bad that I kind of want to find out? Yes, yes, it's very bad. Got it. I promise, I won't think that thought again.

He shows me all the cool things about this place, and trust me, it is very cool. I mean, the way the machines pump liquid gold really gets my adrenaline flowing. Or maybe it's the way Ellis leans against the stainless-steel tank, arms crossed, and green eyes stuck to me.

"This is where the magic happens," he says.

"How exactly do you make beer?"

"Well, it starts with barley. We use a mixture of barley and wheat and then throw a little oat into the mix. Shh, old family secret."

"My lips are sealed."

"Then we add hot water over here." He shows me the machine where it all begins. "It's almost like porridge." His knowledge makes him more attractive. He's not just a pretty face, dammit. "Once the mash is at the right temperature the sugar is extracted. Then from there we add hops and there's a little more to it, but that's the gist of it all."

"Very impressive."

For the next thirty minutes, he leads me around, explaining all the different types of hops and beers they make.

"So, that's the whole place. There will be a quiz to see if you were paying attention," he jokes.

At least I think he's joking, until he continues, "What's the name of this tank?" He thumbs over his shoulder.

"Bob?" I guess.

He laughs. "Someone wasn't paying attention."

He slips his hands into his pockets, and how can you pay attention to someone when all you can think about is that same person putting their hands all over you? Hard to do, huh?

Well, that's me. My whole brain is all disjointed, and all the normal thoughts I should be having about boilers, kettles, and kegs are replaced with sexy images of Ellis while he pours beer over me and his tongue drags down my neck, licking it off.

"Sure, I was," I pipe out.

"We also have a little pub around front. Want a drink?"

"Yes," I say, a bit too eager. "I could really use one."

He leads me back through a door and down a narrow hallway. "What do you think of the place?"

"I love it."

He opens another door and leads me into a dimly lit pub with a few people drinking at the bar.

When I turn to head in the direction of the bartender, Ellis touches the small of my back, gently, and leads me toward a secluded booth in the back.

With sweaty palms and a racing heart, I slide into the padded leather bench seat. "It's really nice here."

"Let me get you a beer. I have one I think you'll love."

He heads toward the bar, and moments later returns with two foaming mugs of beer. My mouth waters as he places one in front of me.

"It's a tropical pale ale. Similar to the I'd Tap That, but it has passion fruit and grapefruit peel with an earthy kick to make it melt in your mouth."

I take a sip, savoring it. "Ah, this is amazing."

"It's all in the hops," he says with a wink. "It's called Luau."

"It's delicious." He sits across from me. "Why don't you work here?" I'm guessing it has to do with his father, but I want to know more. I want to know it all.

"I run the packaging and distribution in Atlanta."

"And you love it?" I sound like a twitterpated school girl.

He takes a swig. "I've been making beer before I was old enough to drink it. My father used to bring me and my brother here when we were kids, and we'd watch him." He looks out at the large space. "Of course, back then, this place was a lot smaller."

"Your dad did good."

"Back then, my father was such a hard worker. He loved the business and everything about it." He takes a drink. "And we idolized him."

"I'm sorry it all changed."

"It's fine." He shrugs it off, like a coat that's not needed. "So, this is the dream my father built."

"Is it your dream?"

His beer halts on the way back to his perfect mouth. "What do you mean?"

"Well," I take another sip of liquid courage before continuing, "your father started this place. Is it something *you* want?"

His brows rise, and I may be overstepping my place here. "Damn," he murmurs, "no one's ever asked me what I want before." He leans in. "It's probably not a good idea to tell you the answer."

"What do you want, Ellis?" I press, my voice dropping a few octaves—not of my own volition. It's the beer's fault.

He doesn't answer, but the flames of desire climb to a cataclysmic level inside me. I can't break away from his gaze.

"You," he finally breathes out.

My thighs clench together as if they can stop what's happening. I am irrefutably turned on.

By another man.

I drain the rest of my beer, so I can keep my mouth busy

and stall a bit before responding. It is so, *so* wrong that I liked hearing him say he wants me. Even though it can never go anywhere. "You can't say things like that to me, Ellis."

He trails a finger against the lacquered wood of the table. "I know. I just can't seem to help myself."

"Well, try," I half-ass say, because I'm sure failing at it. "Henry is your friend."

He scrubs a hand down his jaw. "Maybe we should call this a day."

I force myself to stand. "I think we should. Thank you for everything today." Even though no part of me wants to leave right now, I urge my feet to move. "I'll see you."

I need to get home, where I can relax and think.

I need a bath.

I need a cigarette. Just kidding, I don't smoke, but if I did, I'd probably smoke a whole pack right now.

I just need an escape.

I walk away, not even waiting for his goodbye.

———

MY HOT BATH is not helping me get rid of this tension coiling my muscles into pretzels. Bubbles are bubbling all around me, and I've even lit a few lavender scented candles, but I'm unable to relax.

No matter what I do, I can't get Ellis' hooded green eyes out of my mind. The way he stared at me, shooting flames of heat in my direction when he whispered, 'you.'

It sends chills skating all over my heated skin every time I think about it. I shouldn't be engaged.

I was so sure about everything when Henry asked me to marry him, but now I'm not so sure about anything anymore. What's wrong with me?

Halp. I'm falling for the best man in my wedding.

I sink under the water, letting the silence encase me, thinking about everything I want in my life. What do I want?

Expanding my business.

Happiness.

Ellis.

Pure and simple. That's about as long as I can hold my breath, so I emerge from the water, like a phoenix ready to be born again. Like a woman with a purpose.

"Kiki, are you home?" Henry's voice calls from the front door. I jump, sloshing water onto the tile. "I used the key," he says.

I grab the plush white towel from the railing and hit the lever to drain the water. My heart beat hammers away inside me, giving me new courage to face the things that will be most troubling.

Like facing Henry.

"I'm just in the tub. I'll be out in a minute."

After a quick dry of my hair, I dress in blue-pajama pants and a black tee. It feels like an elephant is standing on my chest. I can barely breathe, but I have to do this. There's no way I can continue to plan a wedding if I'm not sure I even want to get married. When he asked, I definitely wanted to, but now I know I don't.

Why is life so hard?

I wish I was a dog.

Life is so easy for them. Look at Georgia. She didn't care if she married Ace or not. It's hard being a human. There's just something inside me that won't let me go through with the wedding. Is it because of Ellis?

I don't know.

But, what I do know is I'm not calling off my wedding *for* Ellis. I still have no intentions of dating him. I mean, what would be the point? His life is in Atlanta, and mine is here in Florida. Sometimes, they say people are brought into your life to help you find your way.

And I think that's all Ellis is for me.

A compass.

One thing I know for certain—I can't go through with this wedding. Ellis or not.

Henry isn't the one. I don't love him.

I take a deep breath, knowing I'm doing the right thing.

"Henry," I call out, padding down the hallway. "We need to talk."

I find him in the living room, sitting on my couch, one arm resting along the top. He flips through the channels on my TV. "What's up?" he asks, raising a brow.

I sit next to him. "Henry, you're a great guy," I say softly, as if that will somehow keep him from shattering like thin crystal from the heavy blow that's coming. "When you asked me to marry you, I was thrilled. I thought it was everything I'd ever wanted. I believed you and I could be happy. That *I* could make you happy." I pause, clutching his hand in mine. "But, I don't think I can make you happy, Henry."

"Wait." He lets go of my hand, so he can run it over his goatee. "What are you saying here?" His eyes grow wide, like he's just figured out exactly what I'm saying. "Are you breaking up with me?"

"Henry," I don't know why I keep saying his name, "I'm sorry. I can't marry you." I slide the engagement ring off my finger. "I really think you're great. I'm just not the one for you."

"Hold on. I think we can make this work. So, what if you think we're not made for each other. Who is?"

I blink. "Henry, you deserve someone who can make you happy."

"I *was* happy," he states, rather loudly, clearly losing his cool. I don't blame him. And now my heart cracks a little more for hurting him. "Are you feeling ok?" he asks. "Maybe you should sleep on it."

I shake my head, still holding onto the ring. "I have thought about it."

Henry stands. "No, no no no no," he repeats. "This isn't good for my partnership."

"What do you mean?"

"The firm," he whispers, staring off into the unknown. "Never mind." He focuses his dark eyes back on me, "It's ok. Listen, what can I do to change your mind? We've already told everyone we're getting married. Preparations have been made."

I remain seated on the couch, watching as Henry paces the living room floor, and then pulls his phone out to answer a text. "Henry, I'm sorry but…"

He crosses his arms. "We can't call off the wedding. I've invited co-workers."

"We don't love each other." This much is obvious the longer we talk. He's more occupied with what his partners at the firm will think than anything else. "Henry, my mind is made up."

He stands, taking the ring in his hand. "I'll give you some time to really think about this." He moves toward the front door. "This isn't over between us." And then he leaves.

I blow out a long breath, mumbling to myself, "It is, though."

Not once did he say he loved me. And I'm ok with that.

ELEVEN

Ellis

NEVER DRUNK dial someone else's ex...

"EXPLAIN IT AGAIN," my father says. The crow's feet extending from his green eyes deepen as he tries to pull his face into a tight smile. "What do you mean the company is in trouble?"

I lean my arms across the table, joining my hands together. "What Urban told me is that you've gone and gambled away all the money."

My words cause him to flinch. He adjusts the silver tie that matches the flecks in his hair before taking a bite of salmon.

"Must you be so uncivil all the time?" Yasmin pipes in. "We haven't seen you in ages."

"It's not like we're a big 'ol happy family," I say to her. This time she flinches.

I know any normal person would love to spend time with

their father they haven't seen in years. They'd be excited to have dinner with their father and his wife. But, I'm not.

Urban chimes in, "Look we can all sit here and be mad at each other all night long, or we can work together to try to salvage what's left of the family business." Urban pulls a file from his briefcase, spreading out a worksheet with last year's earnings on the table.

I glare at my father. "Do you have anything to offer? Sacrifices to make?"

He stiffens. "I have a certain lifestyle I need to uphold. I can't let people think our business is in trouble. I'm the face of this company."

Yasmin is tight-lipped, knowing her days of drinking wine with the ladies at the club and gossiping about their husbands may soon be behind her.

"Face of the company, my ass," I blurt out. Is he delusional?

"Dad, I called Ellis because we could really use his help. If anyone can pull us out of this mess, it's him," Urban tries to gain hold of the fight that's brewing here at this expensive membership only clubhouse. "We need big changes. Yasmin no longer getting her weekly mani/pedis isn't going to change anything. We're on a downward trend. We need to think of something to bring this brewery back."

The table falls silent as a waiter refills our waters.

"I'm ready to work," I tell Urban.

We need big ideas, but unfortunately the only idea I have centers around a sexy little brunette with the cutest smile I've ever seen. Kiki.

I haven't been able to stop thinking about her all day. And more than anything I want to see her again.

Soon.

But, I know I can't. She's engaged, and even if she wasn't, my life is all over the place.

I need to focus on the brewery, not a hot piece of ass. Don't call her that. She's so much more than just a piece of ass.

She's the marrying type. Just look at Henry.

He knew that, he snatched her up, knowing full well she's indeed the marrying type. I hate it. I've never in my life been put in this type of situation. It makes me think that I *am* the bad guy here. Because every thought I have involves Kiki and Henry breaking up, and me getting the girl.

I know, there's something seriously wrong with me. I can't keep my shit together when it comes to Kiki. And I can't stop thinking about the way her lips felt against mine.

"Ellis," Urban says, bringing my focus back to the meeting. "Do you think you could hit a few restaurants? See if they may want to carry our product? I know if anyone could sell our beer, you could."

I nod. "Absolutely."

"Maybe we need to run nightly specials," my father offers, his smile hopeful.

Urban shakes his head. "I've been working with the bartenders on implementing maybe a two-for-Tuesday deal and some other fun promos. But, the problem is we're just not getting enough people to the pub."

I scrub a hand down my jaw. "So, we need to bump up marketing."

"We have a very small budget." Urban points to a figure on the piece of paper. "We need more organic traffic, and that's why we're failing."

Organic traffic isn't easy to come by, but I may have a few tricks up my sleeve.

The dinner comes to an end, and I shake my brother's hand, leaving my father and Yasmin with no more than a simple 'bye.'

As soon as I walk out of the high-priced golf club, my phone dings with an incoming text. It's Henry, with a 911. He wants to meet at a bar across town.

Sounds important, so I hop in the rental and head off in that direction.

When I get there, Henry's already three sheets to the

wind. "Dude," he slurs out. "I'm so glad you came." He staggers my way, tossing his arm around me. "I've had the worst night."

"Why don't we sit you down." I help Henry back to the bar and the stool he abandoned when he saw me come in. "Two coffees," I say to the bartender. "And a Twist & Stout."

The bartender smiles and turns away to collect my order. I focus my attention back on Henry. "Ok, tell me slowly what's going on? Did something happen at work?"

Henry grabs his drink, which looks like something dark on the rocks, and I try to wrestle it away from him to no avail. Fucker swallows the whole thing. "No," he shakes his head, "Kiki left me."

My heart stops.

"She said it was over," Henry says, looking at his empty glass. "Where's my drink?"

At that very moment, the bartender arrives with both coffees and sets them down in front of us. "Drink this," I tell Henry.

His face is priceless as he stares up at me, blinking like I'm speaking a foreign language. "You serious?"

"Yes, drink this and then you can have another drink." My lie works because Henry takes a big gulp of the first coffee.

"Ow, that was hot."

I push the coffee away. "Next time don't try to chug the whole thing." I grab my beer. "Now, explain to me what happened."

"She left me. Said it was over."

My heart stops again, and I really should have that checked out by a doctor. "Did she say why?" Is it bad I'm holding my breath with the mere hope she did it because she's feeling the same crazy feelings I've been feeling the past few days? Yeah, it's bad.

"Said she didn't love me."

Ouch. "Man, I'm sorry."

"Two shots of whiskey," I tell the bartender.

Henry smiles, his broad shoulders hunched over the bar. "Is one of those for me?"

I crack a small grin. "Drink your coffee and we'll see."

As soon as the whiskey arrives, I knock one back. It burns all the way down and feels so good. I want it to drown all the feelings I have for Kiki.

I take the other shot glass, holding it in the air. "To true love," I say before slamming it back in the same fashion as the first one. I nod at Henry who stares at me like I just stole his favorite kitten. "I'm catching up," I tell him.

He laughs, slapping me on the back. "Two more," he says to the bartender. "Want to hear something crazy?"

"Lay it on me."

Henry sips the coffee. "I wasn't even that sad when she said it. It's like part of me knew what she meant."

"So, it's a good thing then? Keeps you from making the biggest mistake of your life."

The bartender sets down two more whiskeys in front of us. Henry grabs one and downs it. "I'm still going to fight to get her back."

"But, why? You don't love her." I down my third shot of whiskey for the night, utterly confused. Is he just drunk and not thinking clearly? He even said he felt the same as Kiki. So why fight?

"Let me explain something." It's like Henry's sobered up completely as his eyes meet mine. "I'm about to be named a partner." He holds his thumb and index finger millimeters apart. "I'm this close to getting everything I've ever wanted. And the firm favors partners who are settled."

"Settled?"

He nods. "Yeah, as in married. If you can commit to a woman then, in their eyes, you must not be a major fuck up. And it also means someone can stand you long enough to be married to you, so you're most likely a good guy."

"That's bullshit. They can't force you to get married." I hold up two fingers to the bartender, silently telling him we'll have another round. Because I need it. Stat.

"Not forcing. Just heavily implying. The guy who's up for the same partnership as me is about to have his second kid. And here I am, a complete fuck up."

"You're not a fuck up." I brace my hand on his shoulder, giving a supportive squeeze. "You'll find someone."

"No, they loved Kiki."

Interestingly he said 'they' love her and not himself.

"I won't be able to find another trophy like her," he whines, taking another shot glass from the bartender. He downs what I've decided is his last shot of the night.

I stare at my own whiskey, wondering if I should even bother. Listening to Henry talk about Kiki as if she's some prize to be won to help him move up the corporate ladder makes my stomach churn. I nod at the bartender, saying, "We'll tab out."

"No, we can't leave. You just got here, man." Henry's back to slurring his words, and I know I need to get him home before he becomes more belligerent than he already is.

"We'll play some pool." I nod in the direction of the pool tables in the back and pull out my credit card and toss it on the bar.

"I'll kick your ass in pool." As he says the words, two blondes walk by. "Hello," Henry slurs at them. He tries his best to slide off the stool in one movement but stumbles a bit.

I grab him to keep him steady. "Let's go, Casanova."

Once the bartender returns my card, I help Henry to the back of the bar to play a bit of pool, hoping it might sober him up a bit before I get him home.

I rack the balls, and for about a good five minutes we play a friendly game of billiards. Until the blondes head in our direction.

Henry makes an ass of himself, damn near catcalling to get their attention. And my god, it fucking works. I can't believe it.

They join us, and I want nothing more than to bail.

NEVER KISS A STRANGER

Even if Kiki was confused, and maybe unsure if she wants to go through with the wedding, I still feel bad being here as Henry is about to...I don't even know.

I feel like a guilty bystander, watching it all go down—the flirty eyes, the smiles, the way the girls fawn over us.

"Hi, I'm Daphne," one girl says, holding out her hand for me to shake.

"Hey." Every part of this feels wrong, and I don't give her my name.

If Henry wants to fight for Kiki, what he's doing right now with Daphne and the other girl, Melissa...is *not* fighting. But the real sham of the evening is me. Yes, me.

What the fuck am I even doing here? Helping console Henry about his failed engagement while secretly cheering because it has?

It's irritating me how Henry flirts with the two women, leaving me standing here with my stick, trying to concentrate on a moot pool game.

I mean, they just broke up a few hours ago. Come on, man, mourn the relationship a bit. This feels like it's a major disservice to Kiki.

I'd be a wreck. Actually, I am a wreck because I *want* Kiki and can't have her.

The drunk part of my brain is telling me to ditch Henry and rush off to call Kiki and beg her to go out with me. So, I can kiss her again.

The blondes are now playing pool with us, and I try to ward off the octopus arms of Daphne.

"So, you own a beer factory?" she slurs out like I'm some sort of Willy Wonka.

"It's a brewery, and they make the best beer in the world," Henry says, sticking up for my family's *beer factory*, right before he plants a kiss on Melissa.

Should I pull him away? I mean, technically, he and Kiki

broke up. Technically, Henry can do whatever the fuck he wants. And *technically*, so can I.

I should call her.

No.

I line up my cue stick and sink the nine ball, trying my best to not think about how Kiki is now single. She's the type of girl you bring home to meet the family.

If you had a family worth meeting, and I do not. But, she's already met my father, Yasmin, and Urban, so we're ahead of the curve.

Don't get me wrong, Urban is a hell of a guy and definitely worth meeting, but the other two are a hard pass. What am I even thinking about right now? I can't call her. I can't even think about her.

She just called off an engagement.

"Ellis, are you listening to me? Daphne asks, with a scowl on her face.

I scrub a hand down my jaw. "Sorry, I wasn't. What did you say?" I lean an ear closer to her, so I can hear whatever it is she's saying over the loud music of the bar.

"I said, we should get out of here."

I glance over, and Henry is full on sucking face with the other chick. Fuck. Why can't tonight be easy? To say I'm not completely over the moon about the news of Kiki and Henry's break up is beside the point. I can't handle Henry trying to drink and fuck his way into oblivion.

"Henry, I think we should get going." I separate him and the girl. They both react like five-year-old's who were just told Santa isn't real.

I lean close to Henry's ear. "Remember there's a certain someone you want to win back." Why am I doing this?

Pure torture.

"Right," he says, like it's an afterthought. "Yes, I should do that. Will you call Kiki for me?" He reaches in his pocket and thrusts his phone in my face. "Call her. Put in a good word for me." He's all but forgotten the woman at his side.

"*You* should call her. Once you sleep and sober up. Let's get you home."

"No." He presses some buttons on the phone and then hands it over to me.

And it's ringing. And she's answering.

"Hello," I say, "is this Kiki?"

"Yes. Ellis is that you?"

I rub the back of my neck. "Yeah, it's me." And it's at this exact moment the whiskey shots I had earlier decide to take effect. I'm now delayed drunk. "How are you?" I slur out a bit. "Have I been this drunk the whole time?" I muse, not at all meaning to say it aloud. "Shit, fuck, sorry."

"Is everything ok? Ellis are you drunk?"

"It's Henry." I swat my hand at him, trying my best to get his attention away from fondling Melissa. "He called me and we had some drinks."

"Ah."

The background noise of the club fades away as I try to hone in on Kiki's soft breathing. "Are you ok?" I ask her.

"I'm fine," she says with a bit too much chipper in her voice.

I step away from the pool table, scouting out a quiet spot so I can talk to her. My feet lead me outside, where I lean against the wall, letting the cool breeze off the nearby ocean filter over me. "Doesn't sound like you are."

"I'm just confused, ok?"

"Hey, I get it." There's so many things I want to say to her right now. "I get it."

"Do you?" She lets out a huff of air. "Have you called off many weddings in the past?"

I laugh a bit. "Maybe."

"Really?"

"No. When I commit, it'll be forever. No backing out."

"You think I'm awful, don't you?" she questions.

"Not at all."

"Is Henry really drunk?"

I scan the club through the large window. He's stopped making out with Melissa and the three of them are laughing. "Yeah, he's pretty wasted. Don't worry, though. I'm taking care of him."

"You? You sound drunk too."

"I may be a little drunk."

She laughs, and the sound jabs me in the chest.

"Go out with me," I blurt out.

"What? Ellis…"

Before she can shoot me down, I cut in, "I just need to discuss something with you. Over dinner. Or coffee."

"Ok. What about?"

"A wedding for my dog."

"Really?" She pauses, "Um, sure, ok. Text me the details?"

"You got it."

We disconnect, and apparently that saying about being truthful when you're drunk is a lie.

I don't even have a dog.

TWELVE

Kiki

NEVER EAT ice cream out of the carton...

THE DOORBELL RINGS, and I let both Lola and Poppi inside.
We quickly convene in the kitchen where the post-breakup
command center resides.

"I've got Rocky Road and Chocolate Caramel Fudge."
Poppi sets the frosty containers of ice cream on the granite
countertop.

"And I've brought *How To Lose A Guy In Ten Days* and *Love,
Actually*. Which do you want to watch first?" Lola asks, sliding
onto a stool.

"Guys, thank you for rushing over. But I'm fine, really."

Poppi eyes me, carefully. "I brought Kleenex too."

I laugh a little. "I'm fine, really." It's a little unsettling just
how fine I actually am. Even when I sat and conjured up memo-
ries earlier, trying to cry, I couldn't. My tear ducts are broken.

When Poppi broke up with the lawyer she was dating a few months back, she was not fine. We watched three back-to-back chick flicks and ate two pints of ice cream...each.

But this isn't like that. And I really *am* fine. Not like when women say they're fine and they really have fifty million different things going on inside their head.

"So, what exactly happened?" Lola rests her chin in her hand and looks at my ringless finger. "No rock. It's all so real. You sure you're ok?"

"It is real. And yes, I'm fine."

"This doesn't have anything to do with trellis guy does it?" Leave it to Poppi to ask the one question I was hoping to avoid.

"No, of course not." I turn away and place the ice cream in the freezer. While I'm here, I busy myself rearranging some frozen vegetables, so I don't have to face their inquisition.

"Oh my god," Lola exclaims, "it *is* about Ellis the trellis guy."

I exit the freezer and face her. "Can you not call him that?"

Poppi laughs. "Ha. See, we're right. You like him." Her tone is all sorts of accusatory.

"I do not," I lie. "Henry just wasn't the one for me." And that statement is all truth.

"I really thought Henry wasn't perfect for you," Poppi says with a gentle tone. "I figured you'd realize it on your own."

I sigh. "I feel like my body and brain were hijacked temporarily. I didn't really know him when he first asked me to marry him."

Poppi wraps an arm around me. "How did he take it?"

"Said he'd give me time to think." I shake my head, remembering exactly how Henry took it. "I feel horrible. And well, he's so drunk right now."

"Did he drunk dial you?" Lola asks.

"No, not exactly."

Their quizzical looks are almost comical, the way they both

turn their heads, eyebrows raised. "What do you mean?" Lola asks.

"Ellis called. He's at some bar with Henry." There's no way I'm telling them he asked to meet me.

They remain quiet for what feels like an eternity until Poppi finally speaks, "Tell the truth...did you break it off with Henry for Ellis?"

"No." A big no. "I think I just realized Henry wasn't the one." And that's the truth. Ellis may have sped along the process of helping me realize it, but I know he's not the reason. Henry and I wouldn't have been happy if we would have gone through with it.

That answer satisfies them, and that's the end of the discussion. We eat a ridiculous amount of ice cream and watch chick flick after chick flick. And by the end of the night, I know for sure Henry and I would have never made it. I also know I can't wait to see Ellis.

Is that so wrong?

I MAY HAVE OVERDRESSED for this business meeting with Ellis. Or maybe underdressed is a better description. This little blue number held up by spaghetti straps makes my boobs look ten times bigger. I could've easily worn jeans and a blouse, but in my defense, this dress has been collecting dust in the back of my closet for ages now.

When I enter Bearded Goat Brewery, I spy something tall, dark, and panty melting—Ellis at the bar. I bet he's not sweating right now. He's sitting all calm, cool, and collected. Like he owns the place.

Which, well, I guess he kind of does, sort of.

He called me yesterday morning, telling me to meet him here, and I've been a nervous wreck ever since.

I shouldn't be nervous, though. It's not like this is a date.

When he spots me, his face breaks out into an incredible smile. Gah, it's so breathtaking.

"You look...wow," he breathes out once I'm beside him. His eyes scan over every inch of my body, leaving nothing untouched. "Let's get out of here." He waves over his shoulder to the bartender and then places his hand on the small of my back, leading me out of the brewery.

I look up at him. "I thought you wanted to talk about your dog wedding?"

"Yes," he says. "It's a little noisy in there."

Outside, he leads me to the car that destroyed the trellis and opens the door for me.

As I slide in, I'm on high alert for some reason. I almost feel like I'm doing something wrong.

But Henry and I broke up. And you know what else? Once that thought creeps in, it feels normal. Like Henry and I were never *really* a couple. And now that the dust has settled, it's like I can see all the reasons we weren't meant for one another.

As Ellis pulls away, the sun hangs low in the sky, leaving a soft orange glow over the clouds. "I figured we could go to the lighthouse and talk?" He glances over at me. "And then dinner."

"I love that idea." This dress was a mistake. My boobs keep wanting to escape from it—code for it's too damn small—so I keep adjusting it, and in turn, Ellis keeps glancing over at me as he drives the half-mile or so to the Jupiter Lighthouse, centered on the Jupiter Inlet.

"It's getting late, so the number of tourists should be lighter," he tells me, as he parks.

For some reason, I'm happy about that. I want to learn everything I can about the man I can't seem to stop thinking about without distractions.

Waves crash against the rocks lining the inlet as we get out and cross the lot to the red, cylindrical tower jutting toward the painted sky.

Inside, we take the steps to the top in silence. Once we reach the view, it's stunning. It feels like I can see all of Florida from up here. Boats wade in the endless aquamarine water, looking like toys in a bathtub. From way up here, I feel like we're completely alone in this world.

"I've actually never been here before," I admit.

Ellis rests his hand next to mine on the blue railing. "I used to come here a lot when I was in high school."

And I can see why. It's certainly one of the best places on earth.

We watch a few boats speed through the inlet, making their way to the ocean, and then I remember I'm not here to sightsee.

"So, what's your dog's name?"

His eyes dart from the ocean to me. "Spanky," he says.

I laugh. "That's a cute name. What kind is he?"

"A wiener dog."

"You don't strike me as a dachshund type of guy."

"No?" He leans against the rail. "What breed would you think I'd have?"

Under the guise of thoughtful consideration to his question, I take the opportunity to peruse his tall frame from his tousled hair to the sneakers on his feet. And all the lean muscles in between.

"A Saint Bernard."

He grins. "Why's that?"

I shrug. "They're the total package. Smart, good-looking, strong, and loyal. They're a rugged, manly dog."

The tip of his tongue caresses the corner of his mouth and my face heats at the realization of what I just said.

"You don't like wieners?" he says in a husky voice.

"I love wieners," I reply in a hushed tone, barely able to speak. Barely able to stop myself from wondering what his wiener would be like inside me. His dick. Not his dog.

His eyes drop to my mouth and I turn away, toward the ocean.

"The air feels so much cleaner up here," I babble. "Like it has magic in it."

The warm air electrifies around me as he steps next to me. His arm brushes mine and every fine hair stands on alert.

"Do you believe in magic?" he asks, unaware of the spell he's casting.

"Well, I do like Harry Potter." Our eyes meet and he smiles. "God, that sounded so nerdy."

"I like nerdy." His smile fades. "I never asked how you're doing."

"How I'm doing with what?"

"With calling off the wedding. Henry. The whole thing. Your mom."

I bite my lower lip. "I'm actually better than should be expected. Mom wasn't happy." I lean against the railing, mimicking Ellis' stance. "But without a doubt, we were never meant to be together. We just didn't...click. Ya know?"

Ellis nods. "I do."

We stand in silence as the breeze plays in my hair, until I force myself back to business. "Speaking of I do's, should we discuss what you want for Spanky?"

"Ah, yes," Ellis says. "Maybe we can talk over dinner?"

I shouldn't agree to dinner, but I do.

I don't know what it is about this man, but there's something there. Something drawing the two of us together.

We stay at the lighthouse for a few minutes longer before heading to a quaint cafe around the corner. We're seated in a matter of minutes at a wrought-iron table on the patio, over-looking the ocean. The stars twinkle high in the sky as if they're putting on a show only for us.

"May I get you a drink?" the server asks.

"What would you like, Kiki?" Ellis waits for me to answer, unlike Henry who always ordered wine for me.

It feels good to order what I really want. "I'll just have the Guinness."

"Good choice." Ellis winks at me. "Make that two."

After convincing us to order the Cajun chicken sandwiches, the server leaves and Ellis leans in closer to me. "So, tell me all about Kiki."

I laugh a little. "What would you like to know?"

He shakes his head as if I'd even need to ask. "Everything."

I stare into his eyes, leaning forward. "I love the beach and drinking beer." I laugh. "I know, I'm a total Florida girl."

He rests his elbows on the table, adopting my pose. "A total Florida babe."

"Tell me about Ellis?"

He rubs his hand over his chin. "I'm here to help revive a family brewery, but am hoping Henry invests, and I need some kickass ideas."

"Ahh."

Ellis leans back in his chair, and an apologetic smile spreads over his face. "Too heavy for dinner, huh?"

I smile. "No, I guess I asked for it." It makes me feel weird that I'm here with him and he still needs Henry to invest. But, then I remember this is a professional dinner.

The server returns with our drinks and the mood shifts from heavy to light.

"You know what you need," I tell him before taking a sip of my Guinness. "All beers are geared toward men, think about it. Us girls like beer too. Why don't you have something special for us? How about a cool, pink bottle of beer? Or any color?"

Ellis' eyebrow raises as he takes a sip of his dark beer. "Actually," he sets his glass down, "that's a pretty genius idea."

"I'm just saying…"

He prods me for more information about my likes and dislikes, listening as if he's copiously taking notes in his mind. "I'll look forward to drinking it someday," I say with a wink. I have faith in you."

He leans in closer, like he has a major secret to tell me.

"Actually, I've been kind of working on something for a few months."

I place my elbows on the table and join my hands under my chin, scooting closer. "Oh, what is it? Pink beer?"

He leans back, relaxing his posture. "No, it's not that. Well," he bites his lower lip, "it's silly, really."

"Tell me. Please."

He smiles. "Ok, but no laughing."

I giggle. "Promise."

"It's a beer for dogs. But..." he continues before I can say anything, "it's not beer at all, it's a healthy drink with all the joint stuff, and healthy probiotics they need."

I blink at him, suddenly having a whole new appreciation for the man sitting before me.

"That's so clever. What made you decide this?"

"Well, the market is untapped for dogs too. More and more people are including dogs into their daily life outside of the home." He leans back in his seat. "Look at you. Do dogs *really* need to be married?"

I laugh a little. "No, they don't."

"Exactly. So, this is just one of those things."

"I," can't believe this man, "think it's a brilliant idea. Have you told your family?"

He shakes his head, the bright light in his eyes going dim at the mention of his family. "No, I wanted to get a batch together and test it out. Would you maybe want to help?"

"I'd love to help." And then I concentrate on the ocean, to escape the intensity of him. I need to remember why I'm here. This is not a date.

"Are you ok?" Ellis asks.

"Yes." I set my beer on the table, ready to be professional. "So, tell me what you had in mind for the wedding."

He chokes a bit on his beer, and it's my turn to ask him if he's ok.

"Yeah," he answers. "I guess something not traditional? Maybe a beach wedding. The beach is a good place."

My heart stops beating. "Maybe by the turtle sanctuary?"

"Yes, that's perfect."

"Who's the bride?"

He lifts his mug and stares at me over the rim as he takes a long drink. A very long drink. By the time he licks the residue from his sensual lips, I've forgotten the question.

"Angel," he says.

I blink. "Um, yes?"

He laughs a little. "No, her name is Angel." He takes another long drink, draining his beer. "She's a German Shepherd."

"Really?" I laugh. "Well, that's an interesting couple."

"Yeah. Spanky is a stud."

"I bet." Just like his owner. I clap my hands together. "Welp, I have a great idea. Why don't you bring Spanky in for a *Spawesome Pamper Package* so I can meet him?"

"Oh, that sounds interesting."

"It's a great way to relax."

Ellis nods along with me, but he has no clue what he's signing up for.

THIRTEEN

Ellis

NEVER LIE ABOUT A DOG...

"I PROMISE I'm not going to sell your dog," I tell Urban over the phone. I can't back out of the spawesome whatever she called it. "Spanky will love it." Lucky for me, dogs don't talk, because I'm one-hundred percent sure Urban's dog would rat me out about not being his owner.

"This must be about Kiki," Urban says, with too much wisdom for his own good.

I sigh. Maybe I should just come clean with Kiki about not owning a dog. I want a dog—trust me, I love dogs—but working all the time and living in a skyrise with no yard makes caring for one difficult.

"I'll swing by, pick him up, and have him back to you in a couple of hours, and then we can go over business."

"Deal." Urban hangs up the phone, and I grab my keys and wallet off the hotel dresser.

I pick up the dog in record time, deposit his long body in the passenger seat, and head toward the Dog Spaw, looking like a legit dog owner.

I have all the things: a leash, a collapsible dog bowl, and a bag for poop. Not really happy about that last one.

To test things, and make sure we're in this together, I call my new buddy Spanky a few times on the ride over to see if he'll listen to me like I'm his owner. He doesn't.

Perfect.

A dog that hates me.

It's fine. It's not like we'll be hanging out. I'll drop him off for his spa treatment and chat up Kiki while he's being bathed and pampered. He'll be thanking me afterward, because I'm pretty sure Urban's idea of washing this dog is a hose in the backyard.

We pull up to the bright pink building, and I throw the car in park and look into his buggy brown eyes. "You ready for a bath, boy?" I rub the back of his neck while he looks at the building with about as much enthusiasm as a cyborg.

I roll my eyes and open the door. "Let's go, Spanky."

Surprisingly, he crosses from the passenger seat to the driver seat and I help him out of the car.

When we step inside the cool air-conditioned lobby, Kiki waves at us from behind a horseshoe-shaped counter.

Damn, she sure takes the breath away with that killer smile she has.

"We're here for the package," I say, guiding the dog across the tiled floor.

"Is this Spanky?" She moves from behind the counter and bends at the knees to give him a good rubbing down. "He's so cute."

I've never wanted to be a dog more than I do right now. Of course, Spanky loves the attention, lapping Kiki's arms and hands with his wet sloppy tongue. I'd like to lick her too. Oh, the places I would lick.

"Yeah, this is him."

"Are you a good boy?" she asks the dog, and he nips out a little yelp as an answer.

Suck up.

Thankfully, she doesn't ask me, because I'd have to tell her in graphic detail what a bad boy I could be.

She gives him a scratch behind the ears, stands back up, and returns to her spot behind the counter. "Ok, let me just get you guys signed in, and I'll take you both back."

"Oh, I'm gonna go with him?" To be honest, I've never taken a dog to the groomer, but I always thought it was more of a drop off thing.

"Yes, you're both getting the *Spawesome Pamper Package*." Her grin is big. A little too big, like she's holding back a laugh.

"Wait, am I missing something?"

She waves her hand to the wall behind her where a sign hangs, showcasing the details of this so-called *Spawesome Pamper Package*.

I read the first line to myself, and it's a 'doggy and me' grooming package. An owner and dog manicure/pawdicure complete with a blueberry facial.

Nope.

Not today.

"Oh, I didn't realize it was a joint thing." I glance down at my trimmed nails. "I think I'm all good."

Kiki looks at Spanky and parks both hands on her hips, looking sexy as hell. "Do you want a pawdicure with your daddy?"

He yelps out that same barking sound and wags his tail.

Traitor.

"Don't you have some sort of drop off package thing?"

"Oh, come on. where's the fun in that?" She gives me this

slow smile that she hasn't given me before, and I find myself whipping out my wallet to buy anything this girl is offering.

Next thing I know, I'm wearing a paw-print robe over my clothes and reclined in a leather chair with Spanky sitting on a smaller version next to me.

He looks like those dogs on the internet getting the complete spa package, all he's missing is the cucumber slices over his eyes.

He's loving this.

Kiss ass.

"I'm going to do the blueberry facial for you, while Spanky relaxes for a bit."

Music plays in the room at a low volume as Kiki moves to a tall white cabinet, rattles some things around, and returns with a small bowl.

"Be gentle with me," I tell her. And immediately, I envision hard and rough sex. Her bent over this chair with that little sundress pushed up over her ass and my dick sinking deep inside her pussy.

Fuck.

"I have the softest touch in town." I'll bet she does. She sets the bowl on a mini table beside me. "This will be a little cold at first," she says, pressing her hands on my cheeks.

I jolt a little, and not because of the temperature of the paste, but because she's touching me. And it feels fucking phenomenal.

Whisper-soft, she rubs the lotion into my skin, and I close my eyes, because if I keep gazing into hers right now, I may do something we'd both regret—like kiss her.

She massages my face, across my cheekbones and forehead, along the jaw, and I have to say, this is definitely *spawesome*. It's like a perfectly crafted dance. Ever see *Karate Kid*?

The original ones, not the one with Will Smith's kid. Daniel and the girl do this tea ceremony, and it's like the slowest form of foreplay ever known to man.

That's what this is. This is achingly slow foreplay.

But, I'm totally digging it.

I don't dare say a word. I don't even breathe until she stops rubbing and then places a warm cloth over my face.

"Your skin is so smooth," she murmurs, removing the cloth from my face and reaching out to ghost her hand from my forehead to my jaw.

Our eyes connect and there's really nothing in this moment that could make me break this connection.

Except, Spanky. He does that annoying little bark/yelp thing to interrupt the moment and she quickly pulls away.

Jackass.

"So when is the big day?" she asks, moving to a porcelain sink and washing her hands. "We should probably start planning."

"Fuck. Listen, I have a confession." She looks over her shoulder at me. "I don't have a dog."

"Are you ok?" She nearly has a unibrow at this point, but if anyone can rock it, she can. "I'm pretty sure that's a dog beside you."

"He's not mine." And then I keep going, "I kind of borrowed him."

Hopefully, the wrinkle between Kiki's brow is not an indication she's about to bolt from this room. There's no way I can keep up the charade, though. I hate lying to her. I'd have to find a German Shepherd to marry Spanky and it's just easier to come clean. Based on the way Spanky humps everything, I'm not sure he's the marrying type anyway.

"Why would you do that?" she asks, her lower lip jutting out.

"I just wanted to take you out."

She clears her throat and goes through an agonizingly slow process of drying her hands for what feels like centuries before she finally responds, "Take me out? Like a date?"

This girl is so dang pretty it's hard to actually focus on what she's saying. I know, I'm going to Hell. I'm not usually one of *those* types of guys. You know, the ones that can't stop staring at a good set of tits. I've glanced at Kiki's once or twice, but I'm not *leering*.

I'm appreciating.

"Well, going out doesn't need a name." I stand. "I want to get to know you."

And I do. I want to know all about her spa and what she does for fun. I want to know the color of her panties and the sounds she makes when she comes. I'm not going to suggest we label this as friends, because there's no way I'm putting myself in the deathly friend-zone.

"You look really stressed," I tell her. "Want me to give you a facial?"

To my surprise, 'cause I have no idea how to give a facial, she walks to the chair and sits down. "Yes," she says, closing her eyes. "Use what's left in the bowl."

"Look, there's a party at my brother's house," I tell her, dipping my fingers into the goo. I glide it beneath her eyes, like war paint. Her skin is like gossamer as I rub the pads of my thumbs across her cheeks. "You can come and hang out. You have to eat anyway."

"A party. Hm," she muses. "You don't think it's too soon?"

She's not saying no, and I'm taking that as a good sign. "I think time is relative."

"Ok," she agrees, opening her eyes. "We can...socialize."

I trace my fingers around the bow of her lips. "Yes, socialize. I like that."

Now I'm fucking nervous. I don't get nervous. This is my one shot, and why this is so important to me, I don't know.

"Tell me about your business," I say, gliding my fingers along her jaw.

She closes her eyes again and tells me all about how her and Poppi started the Dog Spaw with a small bank loan and a dream. How every bit of their success is because of their dedication to each client. She's smart and that's a big fucking turn on. I'm captivated by her, hanging on her every word.

I think the thing that makes her so damn attractive is she doesn't even know how cute she is. She looks like a blueberry, and I love it. I want to lick it all off her face. God, it's like I've been transported back to high school.

I don't want this to end. For the first time in a long time, I feel grounded.

The urge to spread the concoction across the ridge of her collarbone and onto her breasts is strong, but she puts an end to the facial. "You're really good at this," she says, placing her hand on mine, "but I should get back to work."

Before I can assure her I'm much better at other things, she swings her legs to the side of the chair and stands to grab a towel to wipe her face.

"Ok, Spanky," she says, "your turn."

He wags his tail and I lean against the wall to watch her work.

A popular song pipes into the room—maybe Taylor Swift? —and she sings along as she pampers Spanky.

I smile as I listen to her. "Umm, I don't think that was the actual lyric."

Kiki stops singing. "It totally was. Trust me." She starts singing again, and this time I know she's not saying the right words.

I laugh. "Don't think those are the right words either."

I'm going to be honest, this girl can *not* carry a tune, but she's committed, and I have to give her credit for that.

When Spanky is all done, and his t-rex legs are on the salon door, trying to push it open, I give her the details for the party tomorrow night.

The party I made up. And now, I have to convince Urban to have one.

⸻

"JUST INVITE A FEW PEOPLE," I coax my brother as we lounge

on the back patio of his house that's located along the water. "It's not like you don't entertain here."

Who can blame him? His house is five-thousand square feet of pure relaxation. Boat dock, massive patio set-up with outdoor kitchen and bar, and of course big patio doors that stay open with the soft-billowy curtains flowing in the breeze.

"I don't know," he says with a grin. "I usually only entertain one woman at a time."

I roll my eyes. "I need a party to happen tomorrow night. Do this, and I'll tell you what I'm working on."

"Why don't you just ask her to dinner, like a normal person?"

"It's complicated."

Urban stands from his patio chair and heads to the mini-fridge in his outdoor kitchen to grab another beer. "Why? You said she broke it off with Henry."

I stare out at the water. "I don't want to rush things."

"So, you say." He returns to his chair. "Are you ready to get married?"

I nearly spit out my beer. "Married? We haven't even been on a date yet."

He reclines back in his chair. "Yeah, but it's obvious she wants to get married, right? I mean, she was just engaged. Someone like her is probably expecting you to propose to her after a short courtship like Henry did."

I pull at the collar of my Polo shirt. "Don't talk about her like that."

"Ah," he says.

"Ah what?"

He points his beer bottle at me. "You're already defending her honor."

"Just have a small party," I tell him. "I'll owe you one."

"Oh, you already owe me," he says. "Ok, I'll do it. Now let's talk business. Any updates on Henry?"

"He said he's still working on it." I lean forward and rest my arms on the table. "Is it even going to matter? Does *he* even care?"

"It matters to me," he says.

"Why are we trying so desperately to save something our own father couldn't care less about?"

Urban fixes his hazel eyes on mine. "Listen, forget about Dad. There's other people invested in this brewery, besides him."

He's right. Urban and I both have a lot to lose.

I smile wide. "What do you think about dogs drinking beer?"

FOURTEEN

Kiki

NEVER STOP DANCING...

"HOW DID YOU FIND THIS PLACE?"

"It's the newest thing," Lola yells to me with her boobs bouncing to the beat of the loud techno music pumping from two black speakers not more than ten feet away.

"This is definitely a winner," Poppi says, dancing to the rhythm, amidst the crowd of exercisers.

"I told you, morning raves are the hottest new way to work out." Lola gyrates her hips, sweat already dripping from her brow.

Yes, you guessed it. Lola has struck again. This time, in a warehouse type room with a live DJ on stage, a morning rave erupts around us. The space even has enormous LED screens on the walls and an immersive light display.

Seven a.m. is way too early for this insanity.

But as I glance around, the throng of women clad in workout gear, dancing their asses off, appear to be loving it.

And I have to admit a secret, I'm kind of loving it too. It's a very cool jumpstart to a boring Wednesday morning.

I may not be the best dancer, but these flashing lights kind of put everyone in the room on the same level. This is definitely better than a goat trampling all over me. As the lights change from blue to pink to yellow, I put a little extra sexy in my movements, practicing for the party tonight.

Blue—run my hands through my hair.

Pink—shoulder roll.

Yellow—lower body curl.

"You ok?" Poppi asks.

Blue—hand on my head, chest pump.

Pink—pursed lips, head nod.

Yellow—down to the ground.

"Oh my god, Lola," Poppi yells over the music, "Something is wrong with Kiki."

I pop up from my shimmy. "What? I'm just dancing."

"Oh." She laughs. "Carry on then."

And I do. By the time the class ends, I've got a good handle on all my moves.

"That was so much fun," I say on the way out.

"You looked like you were possessed," Poppi says as we step out into the sunlight. I prefer haunted, but semantics.

Lola smiles. "Maybe it has something to do with her date tonight."

I laugh. "It's not a date."

"Do you plan on talking to Henry about it?" Lola asks.

I nod, opening my car door. "I do. It's only fair. Besides, I still have a few of his things at my house."

We say our goodbyes, and I head home to shower and dress, and then make my way to work.

Once I'm there, I focus on the pups and nothing else. If I

start thinking about Ellis and the party tonight, nothing will get done. So, I won't let myself succumb to such temptation.

The day goes by in a blur of pampering pooches and ends with an inquiry from my last customer about a wedding for her Great Dane. To say I'm excited is an understatement.

"I feel sorry for Precious' husband. She's a real bitch," Poppi mutters as I lock the door. "Who knew dog weddings would become a thing?"

"Yes, isn't it great."

Poppi smiles, but it doesn't reach her eyes, then it turns into a frown. "Should I be upset that Precious can find someone so easily, and I can't?"

"What about the farmer?" I cringe at the reminder of the whole farm slash goat incident. "I thought you had a little crush on him?"

Poppi stares at her pink-tipped nails. "Yes, I did."

"Past tense?"

"Well, we talked on the phone a few times and everything was going great. But then, he never called again."

"Poppi, if a man wants you bad enough he'll make the effort." I smile a warm smile. "Don't stress, you'll find someone soon."

She sighs. "I know, I know. For now, I'll just live vicariously through you."

I laugh, but the laughter isn't real. I don't like seeing my friend upset, and I wish there was something I could do. "Want to eat ice cream?"

She shakes her head. "Promise, I'm not *that* upset."

"Want to go to a party with me tonight?"

She contemplates for a minute, but then smiles. "No, I actually have a good book I want to snuggle up with tonight."

"You sure?"

"Yes, go enjoy your night with Ellis."

I give Poppi a hug. "I love you, girl."

She swats me away, jokingly. "Go, get out of here."

⊏⊐

445 CABANA WAY. See you at 7.

From my car, I read the text from Ellis with Urban's address, to make sure I'm at the right house. The numbers on the two-story monstrous house match, but there are no cars lining the street. Maybe the other guests arrived by boat. The rich can transport themselves however they want.

Part of me thinks I should go back home and cancel this socialization with Ellis, but as I walk the pathway leading to the front of the house, the door swings open. "Hey," Ellis greets me. He grins, effectively shutting down my qualms about being here.

"Hi." I step onto the front porch. "This is a beautiful home."

"I'm glad you came," he says, placing his hand on the small of my back to lead me into the entryway, through the living room, and out onto a spectacular back deck with a view of the water.

"Hello there," his brother says, rising from his seat at the patio table. "There was a little mishap, and I forgot to invite people."

Ellis runs a hand through his hair and looks over at me. "Yeah, looks like it's just us three."

"Well, three is plenty," I say, unsure how you forget to invite people to a party but relieved I don't have to mingle with strangers. Apparently, I only kiss them.

We spend a few minutes chit chatting, and then Ellis says, "I have a surprise for you."

"Should I be nervous?" I tease him.

"You'll see." He tells Urban we'll be back soon, then takes my hand, and leads me down the stairs toward the boat dock. "Urban loaned me his sport fisher."

It's big. It's like a yacht without the fancy title.

As I board, I realize my turquoise mini-dress was a mistake.

The breeze catches the floaty skirt and I have a Marilyn Monroe moment with my ass in Ellis' face.

"Fuck," he grits out.

"Fuck is right," I say back as I attempt to cover my thong. This is how I know for sure I avoided disaster with Henry—I never made an effort with my panties.

When I'm finally on board, I avoid looking at him. But I can feel his penetrating stare as I shrug on a life vest. I'm not required to wear one, but...I feel like I'm drowning.

He steers the boat into the Intracoastal Waterway, stopping to let the boat float in the water, and I peek over at him from my seat. He looks magnificent, like a rogue pirate, with the wind tugging at his dark hair.

"I brought some food too," he says. "Hope you like sandwiches."

I laugh. "I love sandwiches."

He gazes at me with a look in his eyes, that tells me something is on his mind. "I just want to say something." He bites his full bottom lip, and it makes me want to bite it too. "I understand if you want to take things slow. I'm still not really sure what this is, or what this pull is I have toward you..."

I stand, making my way across the hardwood deck until I'm next to him. "Let's not put a label on things. It only complicates everything."

He lets out a deep breath in relief. "I like that idea." He inches closer, his eyes hazy. "You know what else I like?"

"No, what?"

"You. I like that you put this safety vest on, even though if you went over I'd jump in to save you in a heartbeat. I like the way you blushed when I saw your perfect ass. I haven't been able to stop thinking about you since the first moment I laid eyes on you. And I haven't been able to stop thinking about that kiss we shared that day, and how badly I want to do it again."

He leans in, planting his lips over mine, and the next thing I know I feel like I'm floating away on a cloud of lust. Corny, I know, but oh so true.

I cling tighter to him as he deepens the kiss, stroking his tongue against mine.

His hands remove the life jacket, and then explore my back and hips. Somehow, we make our way down into the cabin of the boat still lip-locked.

Things escalate when we end up on a pillow-soft bed. His hands touch everywhere, and then he breaks the kiss, hovering over me.

"Fuck," he groans out. "You make me so hard, Kiki. I've never wanted anyone so bad."

His raw and needy words, spur me to say things I never have, "Touch me, please," I beg.

He presses his hardness into me, and whoa, he's big. He holds his position, not making a move, his green eyes still searing into mine. "I'm going to keep kissing you until you're moaning out my name when you come."

"Promise?" I challenge, feeling more confident in his arms.

He smiles, slow and steady, like I've just said everything he's ever wanted to hear. "I promise, and just so you know, I never make promises I can't keep."

My breath hitches. This man means what he says, and I'm ready to find out if it's true. He presses into me, and I feel like I'm riding a wave that doesn't break. It's incessant. Dizzying. He's really rocking my world. And if it doesn't stop, I might just...puke?

"Ellis," I say against his lips.

"Mm, I love when you say my name."

The boat dips and sways, and my stomach goes with it. "I think I'm going to be sick."

He stops, but the movement doesn't. "Oh shit," he says. "You're white as a ghost." He pokes me in the belly with his hard-on as he lurches off the bed and grabs a trash can. "Here. Just in case. I'll grab some medicine."

"Thank you," I say, sitting up. Big mistake. I'll spare you the details of what happens next. All I can say is, we get to know each other a whole lot better.

⸺

"I'M REALLY SORRY," I apologize again, for the millionth time. "I've never gotten motion sickness before." Once we're back on solid ground, the sickness goes away in an instant.

And I have to commend Ellis for being a true champ. Other guys—e.g. Henry—would probably just let me be sick in private, not lending help.

And I'm beginning to realize Ellis isn't like most guys.

"It's really ok," Ellis assures me as we walk under the moonlight toward Urban's now darkened house. "He's probably sleeping." I follow him up the stairs and across the deck. "Urban? You home?" he calls out when we step inside the patio doors.

A light flicks on in the kitchen. "Ellll-isss," Urban slurs, stumbling a bit to drape his arms around Ellis. "And Kikikiki," he hiccups through my name. "You're back." He looks at Ellis' bare chest. "Where's your shirt?" He takes his off and flings it. "I don't need one either."

He too has a six-pack. Must run in the family.

"Kiki got a little seasick," Ellis explains. "How much have you had to drink?"

"Not much," he says but the evidence sitting on his kitchen countertop says that's a lie. An empty bottle of Hendrick's lays on its side with another half-empty bottle right next to it. He turns his attention to me. "Are you ok?"

"Yeah," I answer. "The boat is all clean. Ellis took the brunt."

He laughs, bringing his drink to his lips for another swig. "The boat doesn't matter. Kiki, did you know we're going to lose everything?"

Before I can ask what he means, Ellis grabs the drink from his hand. "Ok, there. Let's take this and get you some coffee. I'm kind of becoming an expert at taking care of drunk people."

I spring into action. "I'll make the coffee, if you want to get him onto the couch."

"Smart thinking." Ellis puts an arm around Urban and navigates him into the living room.

It only takes a few minutes for me to find a mug in his cabinets and pop a pod into his Keurig.

"You two make the best couple," Urban mumbles from the couch as I approach.

"Oh, we're not a couple," I say, placing the mug of steaming coffee on the table in front of him.

Ellis' eyes dart to me.

"No, you're a couple," he continues on. "Ellis was just saying he wanted to marry you."

"What?" Ellis says. "Someone's clearly drunk and speaking gibberish."

Urban points at him. "You said you wanted to marry her."

Ellis coughs out a laugh and turns back to meet my gaze. "Pretty sure he's got alcohol poisoning."

"It's ok," I finally find my voice to say, my heart galloping at Urban's words. "I'm not expecting marriage or anything."

"But you were already engaged," Urban slurs once more before passing out.

I cringe.

Ellis rubs the back of his neck. "Um, listen, ignore him. I never said anything like that."

"It's ok. I can only imagine how this must look to him." I sigh, wanting to clear the air. "I wasn't looking to replace Henry."

"I know. That's why I don't want to feel like we're rushing into anything...but, I *would* like to take you out. In a social setting."

Instead of agreeing to more shenanigans, I do the right thing and avoid it, "I should head home. I have an eight a.m. spin karaoke class in the morning."

He chuckles. "That sounds interesting. Where do they even have that?"

"Fab Fitness. You should try it sometime," I ramble to ease the awkwardness shrouding the room. "Not that you need it, obviously." I grab my handbag from the counter. "Ok, I'm going now."

He nods and crosses his arms across his spectacular bare chest. "I'll walk you out."

"No, really it's ok." Because if he walks me out, I might not be able to keep from kissing him again. I move across the kitchen toward the arched entryway and stop mid-stride. "Thank you for holding my hair on the boat."

He grins, and then I rush out before I do the wrong thing and invite him to come home with me.

FIFTEEN

Kiki

NEVER SING KARAOKE while riding a bike...

"YOU KNOW WHAT TODAY IS," Lola sings in the middle of a crowded parking lot with a little wiggle to her hips. "It's karaoke spin class, bitches."

"I'm not singing," Poppi says, tossing a white gym towel over her shoulder.

"I'm with Poppi," I say. "I am *not* singing today."

There's no way I can concentrate when my mind is still on Urban's boat.

"You have to sing," Lola pouts as we approach the gym doors. "What's the point of even being here then? We could just go to a regular spin class."

Poppi's lips twist into a small smile. "Fine, I might be able to be persuaded to carry a tune before breakfast. But, no Lady Gaga."

"It's like you're literally trying to ruin my life." Lola opens the glass door, and we follow her through into a glassed area filled with stationary bikes.

"I draw the line at Lady Gaga. Sorry, babe," Poppi says.

As we select our bikes off to the side of the six rows, a voice says behind me, "I think that one is mine."

I turn around to see Ellis in black gym shorts and a Bearded Goat Brewery t-shirt smiling at me.

"Ellis, what are you doing here?"

"You invited me." Poppi and Lola give me major side-eye. "Hi, ladies," he greets my friends.

The conversation is cut short when a lithe woman with a dark ponytail steps to the front of the class. We climb on our bikes as she welcomes us and gives an overview of what will transpire.

"Just look at the screen if you don't know the words," she points behind her. "I'll be coming around with a microphone, so get ready to sing."

Lola laughs. "This is gonna be fun."

I set my water bottle into the little slot on my bike and give Ellis a thumb up. This should be interesting.

The first song starts and Bon Jovi's "Living On A Prayer" Oh good, I don't even need the screen for this one.

Margaret instructs us to warm up and get that blood pumping. Poppi rolls her eyes with a smile and picks up her speed.

I'm trying my best to concentrate on everything going on around me, but Ellis' legs cycling beside me are too distracting.

Margaret zig zags around the room and heads over to me and sticks the microphone in my face. "It doesn't make a difference if we're naked or not," I sing with a blush, before belting out the chorus.

In my peripheral, Ellis' head snaps to me. He grins as Margaret moves on to Lola.

"That's not the lyric," he says, "but I like your version better."

What? I look at the words scrolling on the screen as Margaret continues moving through the class. And oh my god, I was today years old when I learned he's not saying 'naked.'

Sweat beads on my forehead, and I can feel the blood pumping. I'm not sure if it's from cycling or having Ellis next to me. He even sweats sexy.

When Margaret finally sticks the microphone in his face during "Girls Just Want To Have Fun" he very charmingly says, "Oh, no thanks. I'm good."

I laugh. The fact he even showed up here is worth something. So, I'll let him slide on not singing. Forty-five minutes later, we end the class on a Madonna number, and I laugh as Poppi carries out the last note. She can't lie and say she didn't love this. I know her, she did. We all did.

"So much better than goat yoga," Poppi says as we leave the spin class room. "What did you think, Ellis?"

"It was different," he says, opening the door for us.

As people file out into the parking lot around us, I don't know how to leave. What are the rules here? Do I just say bye? Because I want to flee from the man currently charming my friends. He saves me from the awkwardness. "I should get going." He looks down at me with promise in his eyes. "I'll talk to you later."

"Thanks for coming."

"Wouldn't have missed an opportunity to see you singing on a bike." My eyes are stuck to the motion of him raking his teeth across his bottom lip. I feel like he just undressed me in front of my friends. After a quick goodbye to Lola and Poppi, he turns and strides across the lot.

"Things are getting pretty serious with Ellis the trellis guy, huh?" Lola asks.

I frown a little, wanting things to be forever kind of serious with Ellis, but knowing they aren't. "I don't know," I say to them.

"What's wrong?" Poppi asks as we make our way to our cars.

"It's just...I know he'll be leaving soon."

Lola wraps an arm around me. "If it's meant to be, it'll all work out."

I hate when people say that. I love Lola, but I feel like sometimes you have to make things happen, and I'm not so sure if I should.

<hr>

"MEET ME AT THE PIER," a text from Ellis reads, after I'm home from work the next day. "Wear a swimsuit."

I quickly tap out a reply. "Ooh, this sounds interesting."

"I promise you'll love it."

Using the excuse that my couch won't miss me to justify how I didn't even contemplate saying no, I hustle to my bedroom and change.

When I arrive, a shirtless Ellis, wearing black swim shorts, stands on the beach with two surfboards lying by his feet. "Hey, ready to surf?"

My toes sink in the warm sand as I walk closer. "Um, I've never surfed before."

He laughs, looking just like a Greek god out here in the sun. "I did cycling for you. I figured I'd show you one of my favorite workouts."

I smile. "Ok, let's do it."

Ellis studies me for a second before moving a board closer. "First thing you need to know about surfing is balance. Can you balance?" His eyes roam over my body.

"I can balance a goat on my ass."

"Touché." He stares at me. "I just want to say I'd pay good money to see that."

"It wasn't easy."

"I bet." He smiles. "And the goat looked like Henry too. What a weird thing to picture."

I laugh.

Ellis turns serious. "What kind of animal do you think I look like?"

"Hmm…" I study him. His eyes are darker today, the green turned to almost black. "Panther," I whisper. "Because you stare at me like you want to eat me."

He steps closer. "Maybe because I do." A family strolls by, dousing the flames between us. "We should get started," he says.

"I agree." It's a good thing too, because I would have probably let Ellis do anything to my body right here on the beach.

Given the large number of people here, that would probably be frowned upon.

I remove my sundress and Ellis sucks in a deep breath.

"Damn," he hisses, his eyes searing the fabric of my blue and orange bikini.

He gives me a few pointers on how to properly duck dive, pop up, and how to get my footing secure. And after listening to him speak about surfing for a few minutes, I can't wait to get started.

"We'll start easy. Just get you out there and comfortable with the board and waves."

"Ok, I like that."

"So, we'll swim out past the break, and see if we can't start off with a few small swells to get you started."

I smile. "Sounds great."

The waves aren't crazy big here on the east coast of Florida. At least not today.

We wade out into the cool surf, both of us holding onto our boards as we head further out into the deep blue. Ellis pops up on his board and has a seat, straddling it. I follow suit.

"Now what?" I ask.

"Now we wait." He glances back to check the activity of the waves behind us.

I turn my head to take a look at what he sees. "Anything good?"

He smiles. "Not yet, but there will be."

"Did you grow up surfing?" I ask, as we wait with the sun beating down on us.

"My brother and I used to come out a lot after school when we were younger. Before we got cars and discovered girls."

I laugh. "Ah, did you date a lot in high school?"

He shakes his head. "Not as much as my brother did. I had a few girlfriends, nothing too serious. How about you?"

"Well, I grew up here in Jupiter, had maybe one boyfriend in high school. But, I never had anything too serious until I met Henry."

"How did you get into dog grooming?" he asks, dragging his hand through the water.

"Poppi and I worked for a dog groomer, and he was selling his shop, so he could retire. So, we made the leap." I sigh. "I love dogs."

"I've noticed." He grins. "But you're right, that is a big leap."

"Must have been the same for you when you left Florida to move to Atlanta."

"Yeah." He peeks over his shoulder once more. "Here comes a wave. Now paddle with your arms and then hop up onto the board like I explained to stand."

He makes it sound like there's no way I won't accomplish this. Sure, I've seen surfing movies. And sure, in theory it all looks very easy. In fact, I know I've got the gist of the idea down. But, it's the physical aspect of the whole thing. Even though I'm paddling as fast as I can, getting past this wave feels almost impossible.

"You got it," Ellis encourages. "Now get up on the board."

I try. And I do *not* succeed. Although, I'm having a blast.

Ellis lands the perfect wave and makes it look effortless.

Sometimes, things come easily to people. Like Lola and fitness. Or Poppi and sarcasm.

Some of us have to work for it. I give it everything I have and make it up onto the board.

Ellis cheers as I ride out a small wave.

On the beach, he picks me up and spins me around. "You nailed it." My body slides down his as he sets me back on the sand. His eyes penetrate me, making me want so much more of this man. "So, I have something to show you."

I smile wide. "What is it?"

He throws on a t-shirt. "It's at the brewery." He pauses. "We could meet there later, after we go home and shower."

Another idea forms in my head. "Follow me home."

SIXTEEN

Ellis

NEVER TURN DOWN A SHOWER...

MY HEART RACES as I follow Kiki back to her house.

It is so on.

We pull into her driveway, and we make our way inside her place. Her eyes search mine, and I see something I've never seen in any other woman before.

Something...*more.*

Things slow and speed up all at the same time. She lifts her dress off in one fell swoop and tosses it onto the floor. Her bikini is next to go.

This is the first time I've seen her with nothing on, and oh how appreciative I am.

She watches me study each and every curve. I'm a voyeur of sorts, learning the craft as I stalk her with my eyes.

I could stare at this girl all night long. Because it's not just a stare—it's a promise. Of dirty deeds yet to come. Of sweaty bodies, passion, and the type of hot sex you could only dream about.

She turns on the water, and I nearly buckle when she steps inside, curling her finger to me, begging me to join her.

Oh yeah, I'm on my fucking way.

She grins a sexy type of grin, and I wonder how she wears sex and sin so damn well. I don't know the answer, but I want to find out.

I need to find out.

I remove all my clothes as if they're on fire, grabbing a condom from the pocket, and enter under the hot spray with her.

She takes my hand, dropping some soap into my palm and pushes it onto her breasts. "Wash me."

I like a girl who goes after what she wants. She knows herself. Knows what she likes and how she wants it. And I find that type of sexy confidence downright appealing.

I move my hand along her neck, down her throat, between her breasts, and across her collarbone. "Turn around."

And when she does, I make a path over each shoulder blade, down her spine and to her tight ass cheeks. There's something so wildly intoxicating about touching her.

I run my hands back up her neck, moving her wet hair off her shoulder as I peck a soft kiss there. I take a bite over her hot skin, and my dick presses against her.

She lets out a moan, a precious sound, one that makes my cock go from semi to solid in a mere second.

This woman's doing something to me, heating me up all over, and making me know without a shadow of a doubt that I want to be in her orbit. I already constantly gravitate toward her whenever she's around, and right now is nothing different.

It's lust combined with desire and a dash of frenzy mixed in, all rolled into this euphoric feeling coursing through my veins. I bite her skin once more, hoping she rewards me once again with the sweet sound of her moans.

She does.

My heart rages, it's beating to try to catch up with this feeling invading my system. I'm more alert now, more aware of her body than I've ever been before.

She turns, her eyes traveling over me. She takes me all in. Now it's her turn to study, to learn, to figure out what I like and how I want it.

She palms my dick, making me do my very own type of moan. Like I said, I love a woman who takes what she wants, and this girl surprises me at every turn.

She fists it, up and down, pumping it before bringing it closer to her center.

And now it's my turn to be in charge. I spin her, bending her over just a bit, spreading her ass cheeks with both hands.

She spreads her hands against the tile, and I place one hand alongside hers. I run my other through her wetness, feeling her pussy soaked and ready for me.

I kiss her neck, nibbling, sucking, and loving the taste of her skin. "I want to hear you scream."

She glances back at me as I roll a condom down my cock. "Because that's what gets me going. That's what makes me harder than iron. It's what makes me come until I see stars. Knowing I'm fucking you like you need to be fucked. Like you've always wanted to be fucked." By the time I finish my little speech, Kiki's mouth hangs open.

"Oh damn," she breathes out.

I place a finger under her chin, bringing her gaze to mine. "I'm serious, Kiki. I'm not going to stop until my name is echoing off the tiles."

She nods, and I kiss her lips. Long. Smooth. A type of kiss that shows I mean what I say.

"There's nothing hotter than having you soaked and ready for me."

She brings my hand down to touch her pussy, and I slide my fingers through her wetness, before easing my dick inside.

She moans.

I push in deeper, her tightness taking me in inch by inch. Her body comes alive under my touch, her voice going a little husky, "You're such a turn on," she tells me.

"How so?"

"Just how confident you are with my body. How you know that you'll make me scream your name."

I thrust inside her further, faster. "Won't you?" I already know the answer by the way she pushes herself against me. Like she's craving it, and she is.

Hungry.

Desperate.

Needy.

And her body begins to unravel. "Yes, oh god, yes."

"Wrong name, sweetheart." I push harder, slamming my cock inside her from behind, squeezing her ass with my palm.

I yearn for this girl. In my hands. My chest. My dick that's hammering deep inside her. I want her so damn much, so damn bad. I don't want this night to ever end.

The water sprays over us, binding us together in our own little paradise. Hidden from the world.

It's dark. It's discreet. And it's oh so naughty. I can't stop thinking how this girl turns me on so much.

It's in her kiss.

In the way she moans my name.

In the way she pushes her ass against my front, letting me slip in even deeper. God, she has no clue how hot she is. And that's what makes her all the better.

We both groan out together because this all feels so fucking good. It's electric. It's cosmic the way she knows exactly how to turn me on.

"Ellis, don't stop."

"I don't plan on it." I thrust harder. "You turn me on so much."

And she moans out another "Ellis," before her cries turn to pure sounds, so carnal, so wild, so feral. Like she can't get enough of everything I'm giving to her.

She's screaming now, at the top of her lungs even as she yells out my name.

I just go harder, if you can even imagine, and she doesn't let up.

"Do it just like that till you come," I tell her, slapping the soft, wet skin of her ass cheek. "Keep saying my name."

"Ellis, oh god. Yes."

I dig my fingers into her heated flesh, so slick, so wet from the spray of the water.

Her cries of ecstasy overrun the sound of the water, and the steam captures us together, not letting us go anytime soon.

Which is ok with me. Hell, I welcome it.

"You have no idea what you're doing to me."

"You do the same to me," she says. Like she too can't believe what the fuck is happening between us.

I'm fascinated by her.

Like when I kiss her shoulder, she shudders. And when I run my fingers down her spine, she arches back. And when I bring my hands to fondle her breasts, she leans her head back on my shoulder, moaning out long and hard, that she's never been fucked so good.

Yeah, she said that to me.

And yeah, it makes it almost impossible not to come right now.

"I want you to come all over me. Just like this."

My world spirals into a blur of pleasure and desire. Into a whirlwind of frenzied movements and hot flesh on flesh. Sounds echo off the tile in the bathroom, a concert of moans, groans, and growls coming from us.

At last, her body does one last shiver before she cries out a crescendo of unintelligible words, over and over, as her orgasm courses through her body.

She visibly relaxes, but I won't let this be over anytime soon. I want to see that again. "I loved watching you come, and I need you to do it all again."

I pull out of her, spinning her to face me. And then I hook her leg with my arm and slam back inside her, gripping a whole handful of ass.

It's chaotic. It's pure bliss. And it's like the temperature has been turned way up as I continue making this woman feel so good.

And she does. She feels so *so* good.

Her hands fly through my wet hair, and then she cups my cheeks, her eyes meeting mine. "I don't want you to stop."

A warmth spreads through my chest, and I want her to expand on her words.

Stop fucking her. Not even close.

Stop being near her every day. No fucking way.

She kisses me, hard on the lips, and it turns to slow and sensual in a few seconds flat. And with her kiss, our pace stalls, and our movements become unhurried, unsteady, but my heart beat hammers on.

This slow fuck does more to my system than screwing her hard and fast did five minutes ago. I'm so close to losing my cool. So close to fucking coming before I've yet to see her do it again.

"You need to come, Kiki. I don't know how much longer I can hang on."

She stares into my eyes, like she understands my plea, and leans her head back, eyes closed as the water sprays over her.

I lean in, kissing a trail up her neck, biting her flesh, sinking my teeth into her. "Come for me."

Her moans start up again, louder and louder, like thunder crashing all around us.

And my fucking god does she scream my name at the top of her lungs. My girl's loud, and I love every sound she makes.

My body can barely hold on, but I don't let go of her, running my hand up her torso to wrap my fingers around her long, wet hair. I fist through it, pulling her toward me to press my lips against hers. This girl...fuck.

I'm planted deep inside her and already I'm thinking about when's the next chance I get to fuck her. When I will get to have this beautiful woman all to myself again.

I can't stop thinking about the way she feels, or the way she *makes* me feel as I keep screwing her against the bathroom tile.

"I'm going to come...*again*," she calls out for only me to hear, and I wrap my fist tighter in her hair, pulling her forward so I can get a good angle to plunge even harder into her.

God, she makes me come alive. Like some sort of voodoo, I've never felt before.

My heart pounds as she comes all over me.

"Keep coming. Come all over my dick."

The tightness of her as she orgasms spins me into mayhem and my body explodes into hysteria.

After we've calmed, and our heartbeats have returned to normal, I shampoo her hair. She has great hair, and I run my fingers through each strand.

I've got it bad for this girl.

Like really fucking bad.

———

"TRY THIS ONE NEXT." I slide over the watermelon sour beer I've been working on.

She takes the pilsner into her hand, sipping just a bit to let the taste wet her tongue. And this simple action has my dick ready to leave the brewery and recreate the shower we just took not too long ago. "Mmm," she says.

"For that beer, I'd use this bottle." I slide over the graphic I've hand drawn of a rose-colored beer bottle with a pink label.

"Wow." She stares at me like I'm an anomaly she can't quite figure out. "You drew this?"

"Yeah." I shrug. "It's always been a passion of mine."

She takes another sip, and I've never in my life wanted to be the rim of a glass. "I love it, it's all so classy. Not over the top."

I wet my lips. "Yeah, that's what I was going for. But, I have others too." I slide the next coffee and cream flavored porter. "Try this."

She takes a sip. "Oh, I love that one."

"And I'd use this bottle." I show her the graphic of a white bottle with orange and red swirly designs.

She takes a longer beat to study it. "You're so talented." The scent of her coconut shampoo floods my nose, and I'm transported back to the shower with her body against mine.

"Thank you," I whisper out in a rush, trying my best not to kiss her right now.

"So, what happens now? You'll start selling this beer in the pub?"

I stare at the pictures for a second before answering. "I wish it were that simple. I need something bigger. Maybe a launch party to showcase the products. I have a few restaurants to hit to see if they'll carry our beer, as well as seeing if the others who do carry, would be willing to pick up the female beer products."

And now I need to make sure these ideas stick. With me leading the brigade, I'm sure I can convince restaurants they'll want these products.

Every restaurant wants the next big thing. The 'it' beer that'll make the patrons rush to the bar to drink it. It's simple really, we need to make sure the girl beer is marketed just right. As the next 'it' item.

"Ahh, lots of steps."

I can't help but notice the way her eyes sparkle when she

stares at my pictures once more. "Yeah, nothing in life is ever easy."

"Especially things that are worth it." Her words hang in the air.

We're alone in the brewery, thanks to the key Urban gave me, so I lean in, kissing her with abandon before letting her try any more beer.

Before I lose my head and fuck her on the bar, I break the kiss. "Want to try the dog beer now?"

She scrunches her cute little button nose. "I don't know. Is it safe?"

I'm trying real hard not to sweep everything off this countertop, bend her over it, and spank her for thinking I'd give her anything not safe. "Just because it's for dogs, don't think it isn't one-hundred percent healthy for humans too." I slide over the bottle, twisting off the cap for her. "Try this one, it's called Pup Pow."

She tries it and her brows raise. "Wow, that's not too bad. And it's good for them?"

"Yeah. A lot of dogs need joint vitamins, and when they're puppies it's always good to get them on a vitamin regimen." I hand her another bottle with a picture of a dog licking a bowl of beer on it. "This one I did a rough sketch on the bottle label."

She studies the bottle of Doggone Good, and does that thing again, where she stares at me like I've impressed her. "Have I mentioned I love this idea."

I crack a sly grin. "Maybe you should show me how much you love it."

"Maybe one day I will." She stands and walks her tight ass away to check out the machinery.

I watch her like a hawk.

"So, you made all the new beer here?"

I lean against the stainless-steel counter, crossing my arms. "Yeah, I did."

"And now you'll go to Atlanta to make samples to show them off?"

"Yeah, at my manufacturing facility."

"I don't know why I find that so sexy, but I do."

I grin. "Yeah? What else do you find sexy?"

She sucks in a breath of air. I'm kind of anticipating her answer, ready to make sure I do everything on her list. Pending she has a list, that is.

She hmm's and hah's for a moment before saying, in the most seductive voice imaginable, "I find it sexy when you kiss me." She takes a step in my direction. "And I find it sexy when you touch me." Another step closer. "And when you say my name."

"Oh yeah?"

"Yeah," she breathes out.

"Let's get out of here."

She nods. "Absolutely."

Before we can even make it to the back door, Daddy Dearest comes strutting in like he owns the place. And I know he does. He fucking does. Don't remind me.

He stops, surprised to see us. I'm not going to be the first to talk here. In fact, I try to maneuver Kiki around him to no avail.

"Leaving so soon?" my father asks.

"We just have somewhere to be." Like my bed with our clothes off.

"What have you got going on here?"

In my own haste to get Kiki naked, I forgot to put away the artwork for the beer we've been testing. "Nothing."

My father picks up a design and studies the picture. "What is this? Is this a beer for dogs?"

Kiki glances at me. Sure, I'm here to help my father not lose his life's work, but that doesn't mean I'm gonna share all my ideas with him before I even know if they're gonna work.

Hell, I have barely told Urban my plan, all he knows is I'm working on something new.

My father scoffs. "You think the way to bring this company back to life is by giving beer to dogs?" The look on his face shows exactly how unimpressed he is.

"It's actually a bit more than that," Kiki says. "It's pretty genius." I know she's trying to ease some of the tension floating in the air, but it's a waste of her time.

"What's this?" He picks up the graphic with pink bottles. "Is this what I think it is?" He raises a brow.

"It's a beer geared toward females."

Obviously, he's not a fan of these ideas, and I won't let him belittle me, especially in front of Kiki.

"You don't want my help?" I let go of Kiki's hand, leaning against the stainless-steel counter. "I'll go back home to Atlanta and call it a day."

My father stares at the graphics a second time before asking, "Do you really think people would be into this sort of thing?" This time his tone is more thoughtful of the product. Like he might actually be thinking about it.

"I do." I take the pictures from his hands. "And you should too. I'm here to help, nothing more."

I grab Kiki's hand and this time I do make it to the door before my father calls out my name.

I stop, glancing over my shoulder.

"I'm glad you're here," he says. "Truly, I am." All the cockiness leaves his face, revealing just an old man with a lot of regret filling his eyes.

I nod and walk out the door with Kiki.

Not even looking back.

SEVENTEEN

Kiki

NEVER FORGET to answer your phone...

"WHERE WERE YOU LAST NIGHT?" Poppi asks as I stroll into the Dog Spaw early the next morning.

"Ellis took me to his brewery to try a few things." I shrug, like it's no big deal.

Because if I make this into a big deal, it'll escalate into boyfriend territory and then Ellis will think I'm trying to hook him into a marriage. I mean, he has to already be thinking about it, right? I plan weddings. I was engaged.

Two plus two and all that.

I mean, he has to think all I want in life is to wear a white gown and walk down an aisle. But, that's not what this is at all.

I don't feel like I need to get married right now. Sure, I've thought about it. I feel like it's on Ellis' mind too. And I wish there was a way I could get it off his mind. Because I don't want to ruin this thing before it's begun.

Ugh, to be honest, I'm kind of glad he left for a few days to head back to Atlanta. It's a nice break to think. But, that task proves impossible because of the next person who walks through the front door of the Dog Spaw.

"Hi, Kiki. How are you?" Yasmin saunters in and gives me air kisses on each cheek. "It's been too long."

I think it hasn't, but I play nice anyway. "What brings you by today, Mrs. Atwood?"

"Well, I wanted to get more information about your services. I have two Pomeranians. Doodles and Sparkles. And I want them to get married."

She stuffs her hand into her oversized Prada bag, and pulls out a bedazzled phone. She swipes and taps and then the next thing I know I'm staring at two little golden furballs. "This is them."

When Yasmin said at dinner she'd want to talk to me about her pups, I never imagined she'd actually follow through. And I'm thrilled I get to plan another wedding.

I sit Yasmin down at a small table near the front window. "Would you like something to drink?" I ask her.

"Sparkling water, three limes and one lemon. No ice."

I nod and leave her to grab my binder with a few samples and pictures of things I can offer with the dog weddings. Once I've retrieved the big three-ring binder, I make my way back with the sparkling water and take a seat. "Sorry, fresh out of fruit." And that's the truth, we don't keep fresh lemons and limes on hand. Why would we?

She waves a dismissive hand. "Oh, it's fine, dear. Now let's talk about Doodles and Sparkles."

I pull out a notebook and flip it open. "When would you like the wedding to take place and where?"

She pushes her long blonde hair off her shoulder. "Next

weekend at our estate. We have a gorgeous backyard that over-looks the water."

I pick up my phone to check the calendar and my heart skips a beat when I see I've got a missed text message from Ellis. I don't open it and check the calendar for the date. "Ok, that'll be the thirty-first. We can totally do that. Do you have an idea of how many guests there will be?"

Yasmin's face lights. "Seventy-five at the most."

My eyes widen because seventy-five people...for a dog wedding? It's almost mind-blowing. I swallow. "That's quite a lot of people."

Yasmin smiles. "Yes, we have lots of friends with pets. I'm in a Doggy Mommy group in the neighborhood."

I smile, writing down the number.

Yasmin places her hand over mine. "Do you think you could talk to Ellis? Convince him to come? It would mean so much to Doodles and Sparkles."

I bite the end of my pen. I'm sure it's not the dogs who want him there, but I smile. "Ok, sure. I'll try."

Yasmin and I spend the next thirty minutes discussing all things doggy weddings, and the whole time I try my hardest not to think about the text burning a hole in my pocket.

As soon as she walks out the door, I yank my phone out of my jeans' back pocket and open up the messages.

"Thinking about you," is all it reads.

And I swear my heart does some little fluttery-flippity thing.

"SO, you can't stop thinking about me, huh?" I text Ellis back once I get home from work. I kick off my shoes and fall onto my couch.

His reply comes back in an instant, "Yes. All day."

"I've been thinking about you, too."

"Have you missed me?" he texts back.

Honestly the man has been gone for twenty-four hours and yes, I do miss him. Is that too shameful to admit? I'm trying to be casual here, so Ellis doesn't think I'm a psycho-wannabe bride. "Maybe a little."

"Only a little." he replies instantly.

I laugh slightly, my cheeks flaming red. "Ok, maybe a lot."

"Me too. I can't stop thinking about the other night."

"The shower?" Listen, I haven't been able to stop thinking about it, too. Like everything this man does is such a turn on to me.

But, it's so much more than that. At the brewery, looking at how talented he is with his designs. Is there anything this man can't do?

But, is it weird if I say I can almost feel Ellis through the phone. Not physically, of course. But, emotionally. Spiritually. Like there's this intense connection I don't want to break. I grip my phone, waiting for his answer.

"Yeah, you have no idea how hot it was to have you go wild on me like that."

My face flames red, and next thing I know his name pops up on my caller ID. I answer, "Hello."

"Hey," he says in the most sexy, husky voice I've ever heard him make. "I've been thinking about you all day, and I needed to hear your voice."

And at this very moment I realize how good it is to hear his voice. How in some weird way, I've missed it. "I'm glad you called."

"Oh yeah? Why's that?"

I lay back against the couch, my body growing a little needy from the sound of his voice. From the intimacy we're sharing right now. "Because I wanted to hear your voice too," I tell him.

"You sound like you're lying down, are you?"

I nod, even though I know he can't see me. "Yeah."

"I am too."

The image of him lying down, one arm possibly behind his

head, his abs on display is emblazoned in the image center in my brain, not going away anytime soon. I have to be honest, I know where this is headed, and I have a teeny-tiny confession to make. I've never done this before. To be real, I've always been too embarrassed to try. Like it's silly, right? I can't do anything like this, what would I even say?

Ellis answers that internal question for me. "Just let me tell you what to do, Kiki." And he says this in such a low voice and with such seduction I could almost come on the spot for him.

"I'm not really sure what to do."

"Start by telling me what you're wearing."

I stare down at my outfit, wishing I had something sexier on. "Just jeans and my Doggy Spaw t-shirt."

"Are your panties cotton or lace?"

"Cotton," I answer quietly, ashamed of my answer. I wish I was wearing something erotic to turn Ellis on.

But, it doesn't matter because he growls into the phone. The same growl he made when he saw me naked for the first time. "I've pictured you as a cotton girl. Take off your jeans and describe your panties to me."

"Ok, I'm unzipping my jeans now." I can't believe how turned on I am once I discard my jeans and toss them across the room. "They're red with little yellow polka-dots on them."

He hisses into the phone.

And I do something bold, something I never thought I'd do in my life. I line up the camera on the lower half of my body and snap a pic. And then I click send.

"Fucking Christ, Kiki," he says after a minute. "Are you trying to kill me?"

I can't help but giggle a little into the phone. "Did that turn you on?"

He lets out a deep breath. "Just thinking about you turns me on."

"I wish you were here right now."

"Me too, but I can't be. So, I need you to touch yourself like

I would touch you. I need you to be a little rough, and a whole lot gentle. And I want you to tell me exactly how it feels."

"And what will you be doing?" I ask him, too turned on to really think about anything else.

"I'm gonna be stroking my hard cock until *you* make me come." He lets out a deep sigh, his voice a little shaky with desire. "You want to make me come, right?"

More than anything. "I do." My eyes widen as the urge to be touched between my legs becomes too much. I squeeze my thighs together, moaning a little as I do. "I'm so wet," I say as I slip my fingers over myself.

I can't believe I'm really doing this.

"I've got my big dick in my hand. It's so hard, Kiki. You make me so goddamn hard."

"Does it feel good?" I ask him, needing to know. Wanting to know if this is turning him on as much as it turns me on.

"So fucking good. How does your pussy feel?" He groans hard. "I want you to pretend it's me touching you."

"I am." I race my fingers over my clit, loving the pressure of it. "So good, Ellis."

The sounds he makes urge me on, making me roll my fingers over my clit faster and faster. "I'm being rough with my cock. Are you being rough with your clit? Are you treating it like you never have before?"

I push harder against my wet skin. "Yes, I am."

"Good. Keep rubbing. When I get back to Florida I'm coming straight for you."

His persistence turns me on, making me burn with how consumed he is by me. "Please do." I moan louder. "Please, Ellis."

"I'm gonna make you come all over me, Kiki. All over me." His voice shakes a bit, and I'm already seeing stars.

"I'm coming," I cry out as my body spasms through my orgasm.

Ellis' voice growls, a pure guttural sound as he keeps stroking himself. Harder and deeper than it was the other night. Like his own neediness has grown more since seeing me last. This thought drives me through the roof. "I need you to make me come, Kiki. Tell me how badly you want to suck my cock."

I lick my lips, my body still reeling from my most recent orgasm as I whisper into the phone, "I want to take you deep down my throat."

"Fuck," he says on a groan. "I'd fuck your mouth so good." I believe him. And then his moans turn to growls in an instant, and the next thing I know he's making the most sexiest and manliest noise ever. He's coming, and it makes my chest warm as I listen to him.

"I can't wait till I get home," he says before saying goodnight.

And as soon as we hang up, I'm reminded that Florida isn't his home, although he just called it that.

I'm sure it was an innocent slip up, but a small part of me wonders if Ellis is feeling exactly what I am.

EIGHTEEN

Ellis

NEVER STOP LIVING...

AS SOON AS I step off the plane in Florida, the only thing I can think of is Kiki. I've never craved anyone this badly before in my life. Since having phone sex with her a few nights ago it's been on repeat in my mind. Don't get me wrong, I had to go to Atlanta. There was no other way of getting around making the bottles anywhere else. Now I've got the bottles, time to brew some beer to put in them and get them out for testing.

But, none of that is important right now. I don't even stop at my hotel after getting off the plane. No, my mind is in *go* mode. Like a big fucking green light with Kiki.

I should be heading the other way. I should be a good guy, and remember her ex is the whole reason we're getting a second chance with the brewery. And I don't know if he'd be willing to invest if he knew I was falling for her.

155

But, I can't think about any of that right now. I can't think about anything, really.

And if I'm being perfectly honest, I don't think wild horses could stop me from knocking on her door and waiting as patiently as I can for her to open it. And oh boy, when she does, it's an out-of-this-world experience.

"Wow, you look...wow," I fumble over my words.

She laughs a little, and there's a new glow to her. One I'd never noticed before. She looks like sex on legs, some very nice toned legs. Her hair falls down in a waterfall of brown waves, and her dress is some yellow number that displays her tits in the most awesome way. I can't keep my eyes off them. "You too."

"Did you want to grab dinner?"

She shakes her head. "No, not dinner."

I crack a smile. "Dessert?"

She shakes her head again with a big smile.

"Coffee?"

Once more she shakes that beautiful head of hers.

"My hotel room has a hot tub." And that's all I need, and Kiki walks hand in hand with me toward my rental car.

And it is so on. I drive like speed limits are a myth, and pull up to my hotel in record time.

We make our way through the lobby without looking completely awkward. I open the door to my room, and lead her inside.

The hot tub's off a private deck, and I can't wait to get her in there.

I've been thinking about her all day. Like all fucking day long. All fucking week. And I can't wait to slip my cock deep inside her.

Just the thought of it is getting me hard as I open a bottle of wine for her as she stands on the deck overlooking the ocean.

"Beautiful, right?" I ask her, offering her a nice Pinot Grigio.

"I love it here. I wish I could live right on the beach." She turns to face me. "Do you miss it?"

"Miss what?"

"The beach, the ocean."

I shrug. "No, not really. Maybe a little come winter time." I smile, but I know that's not what she's really asking. She's asking if I would ever come back to it. If I'd ever move back here to Jupiter. To be with her.

And honestly, I don't know. I know I really like her. And the way she looks tonight, I know if I left this place I'd miss her every damn day.

"Come here," I say to her.

She crosses the patio, and I step behind her. She leans her head back against my chest, and together we watch the crashing waves along the shoreline.

It really is breathtaking. And my body hardens when she pushes her ass back against my dick.

He's awake, and my body's raring to go. "You have no idea what you do to me, Kiki."

She turns in my arms to face me. "You do the same things to me."

There's a warmth in my chest that spreads throughout my body, limb to limb, igniting a flame of want only Kiki can satisfy. I kiss her. Our tongues mingle. And I keep kissing her as I take her wine glass from her and walk her closer to the tub.

"I need to get you naked and into this hot tub." Like right the fuck now.

Kiki draws in a breath, and kicks off her shoes. That's the right idea.

I set her wine glass down, and rip off my shirt. I turn on the hot tub and wait a second for the jets to start bubbling.

When I glance back at Kiki she's removed all of her clothing down to only her black-cotton panties. She faces me, and I suck in a deep, ragged breath. "You're drop-dead gorgeous," I tell her before unzipping my jeans. "Do you know that?"

She steps closer, her cheeks flaming crimson, putting one

foot into the tub. "Thank you," she says, peeking up at me through her long lashes. "You're not so bad yourself."

I smile, removing my boxers and letting my cock spring to life.

Now it's her turn to gasp when she sees me fist it in my hand. "Get in," I tell her, nodding to the hot tub.

She removes her panties and then steps in, sitting down on one of the seats.

I follow in after her, and sit next to her, my body so turned on more than it's ever been before. "You know what I love about Florida?"

Kiki runs a hand over my thigh, her nails tracing over my skin, creating sparks that fly up my leg. "What?"

"Every day feels like vacation."

She laughs, the sound waking me up to the possibility of hearing it every day. "You're kind of right. Except in summer, when you melt into the sidewalk while walking from your house to the car."

I crack a smile. "I don't miss the summers."

"There's something I've been thinking about all day." She straddles my lap, pushing her tits in my face.

Oh, yeah.

I lean in and kiss her soft skin, making my way over each peak with my mouth before drawing one into my lips, nibbling my teeth over her pebbled nipple. I press my hand against her back, bringing her body closer to me. "What's that?"

She cups my face, like she seems to do a lot. And I'm not gonna lie. I really dig it.

"The way you get so hard in an instant. The way you sound when you come. I can't get the visions of it out of my mind, and it turns me on."

I stall, my eyes searching hers. "You do know it's because of you, right? That you make me so fucking wild with every little thing you do."

"Like what?"

I suck in a breath, like all the oxygen has been pushed out of the air, and I'm left with this sense of loneliness without the thought of having her with me always. "Your lips, for starters. I fucking love your lips. I love the sounds you make when I touch you. You make me so damn hard when you look at me like you're looking at me right now. Like how you looked at me the night you first saw my drawings."

"Like you're a mystery to me?"

"I think I'm pretty easy to figure out." I squeeze her body in my hands.

She shakes her head the tiniest bit. "No, you're not."

I kiss her lips, kissing her the way she deserves to be kissed. She grinds against my dick, and I want to stare at her. To gawk at her. To look at her and never stop looking at her.

"I want you, Ellis," she breathes out, her voice strained as she rocks into me, and by god this girl will fucking have me.

All of me.

My dick turns rock solid. It's go time if there's ever been a go time before.

I gaze into her eyes, staring up at her slightly. "Kiki, you may think I'm a mystery, but I think it's pretty obvious what you do to me. How you make me feel." I grab her hand and place it on my hard on. "This is what you do."

She moans out, hurried, uneven, and the sound of it makes me want her even more. The sexiness of her tone. The want so fucking apparent as she murmurs. I want her. My fucking god, do I want her.

Make sense? Good. Because nothing right now in this moment makes sense anymore. The world has turned topsy-turvy and I can't decipher which way is up or down. All I do know, is there's an electrical current in the air, sizzling between us.

Her hands land on my shoulders, and she nuzzles her face in the groove of my neck. "I'm yours," she whispers against my skin, so feather soft I almost don't hear her.

But fuck me, I'm so glad I do. Because it ignites something deep within me.

It's like a light switch has been flipped on, blazing from the inside out. I don't know what to do with all this brightness, all this energy, so I kiss her. And let me just say, I love kissing her. I really do.

It's slow. It's fast. It's everything a kiss should be, tongues colliding, moans escaping. It's like we can't get enough of each other, so we try harder and harder.

I lean back after I've broken the kiss and reach for my jeans pocket to find the condom tucked away inside.

Because I need inside her now.

"I'm on the pill," she tells me, her big brown eyes trusting me with everything she has.

Oh fuck. "Are you sure?"

She nods. "Yes, I want to feel all of you."

I'm going to let you in on a little secret. I've never gone bareback in my life. Ever. And my heart is like a jackhammer inside my chest, begging me to feel her with no barrier between us.

I push inside her, my mind floored by the sensation, the tightness, the actual fucking feeling of her.

She moves her body down my bare cock. "I love how big you are." She wriggles even closer, her tits pushing against my chest.

I rock up as she moves on me back and forth. "I love the way you feel." And fuck, I'm not lying one bit. "Ride me, baby," I tell her.

Her eyes meet mine, and the next thing I know she's bucking against me, taking my cock as fast and hard as she wants. And I let her. I let her use me to her liking.

And by fucking god is she using me.

She moves and rides, and finds her own rhythm, taking every single fucking inch of me over and over again.

And it's right here and right now that I realize I am one-hundred percent hers.

And I want her to know it. I want her to trust me. To feel good around me.

Fuck Atlanta, this woman is my future.

NINETEEN

Kiki

NEVER DENY yourself what you truly want...

I CAN'T BELIEVE THIS. I can't believe I'm having incredible, mind-blowing sex with Ellis Atwood. This is all too amazing. He feels so good, and the lazy look in his eyes is so sexy I could die.

I move my body against him, riding his dick. It all feels like heaven, and I arch my back, sticking my breasts closer to him.

I know he loves it by the slow smile that spreads over his face. The way he stares at me makes my pulse quicken.

He takes the bait and runs both hands over them, sucking my skin into his mouth. His neediness is a major turn on. Everything about Ellis is a major turn on, but it's the way he stares at me. Like he's studying my body to memorize it.

I curl my fingers into his thick brown hair, pulling just enough to hear him groan out. I love his sexy sounds.

So manly. Such a turn on. And if you want to know what the biggest turn on is, it's his dick. It's perfect in every way.

I know not all dicks are created equal, and believe me, I've seen some less than stellar ones, but Ellis has this perfectly straight and big stallion of a dick.

I swear the God's were shining down on him in the looks and body department. And he scored big time in the personality department as well. An A+ of a psyche. He really is a catch.

The whole package.

I keep moving my body against him, focusing my attention back on Ellis and not the impending dreaded future. I won't focus on it, I'll live in the here and now. Live in this very moment where Ellis is mine, and only mine.

I keep moving, grinding myself against him, loving the way he grips my ass as he sucks on my chest. I lean my head back, the tips of my hair float in the water as Ellis pushes his dick up into me harder and faster. Yes, oh god yes, I'm so close. "Don't stop," I cry out.

He smiles, his teeth grazing over my collarbone. "Don't plan on it."

My body builds, the crescendo so close to crashing down all around me. It all feels so hot, so good. Too much. Everything comes to a thudding halt inside my chest, and it's all like an orbital shift, throwing me completely off my axis. My chest explodes with warmth and emotion, but I keep riding it out, the best fucking orgasm I've ever had.

I can't stop shouting out his name as he takes over and stands me up, he flips me onto my stomach, half out of the tub, with only my legs still in. He pushes back into me from behind and grips his hand around my hip, his other hand tracing up the spine of my back. "I love your body," he says, trailing kisses where his hand once was. "I love your skin."

I moan out, my body still feeling dizzy from my orgasm.

"You're so fucking naughty, aren't you?"

Am I? "How so?"

"Oh, come on, you can't tell me you aren't thinking about me fucking you all day long. Do you think about my cock all day?"

"Yes." I do. "Yes, Ellis."

"Do you think about me fucking you all night long? Wishing for it?"

"Yes, oh god yes." My body builds.

He's still a puzzle I'm trying to figure out.

"You make me want to fuck you every chance I get."

That is definitely not a bad thing.

"You make me want to spread your thighs open every time I see you."

"Yes, Ellis."

"You know what else you make me want to do?" he asks, his body thrusting into me at a rapid pace.

"What?" I ask.

"You make me want to come all over that beautiful face of yours." He bites my shoulder. "You make me want to come all over you."

Goosebumps erupt all over me as he keeps pumping inside me. "Yes, please."

"You make me want to claim you, Kiki. Are you mine? Will you let me claim you?"

"Oh god, yes." I've never had a man talk to me the way Ellis does, and it turns me on so much.

"Do you want me to come deep inside you?"

I cry out a yes, oh my god, yes.

He keeps going, his body as hard as steel. "You're the only woman I want to come inside. The only woman I have ever come inside."

My eyes widen at his words, and I want to look into his eyes when he comes. "I want to see you," I say before turning around and sitting him down, so I can return us to the position we were just in, me straddling him.

He runs his hands through my hair as I sit down on his dick. "You're mine, Kiki."

I nod. "Yes, I'm yours."

He keeps his hands gripped on my ass as he pushes himself up into me, in and out, making me race closer to another orgasm. "And I'm yours," he says, turning my whole world upside down.

"I'm going to come again," I yell out.

He has a small smile and his eyes meet mine. "Come with me?" It's almost a question as his mouth crashes against mine.

God, this man. I swear. He just does things to me. Things no other man has ever done. Good things. Butterflies in my chest good.

Oh, so many good things.

I come again as he grumbles he's so close. And then the most amazing thing happens. He comes, with me holding him tight, and I swear I've never felt closer to another human being in my whole entire life. The connection. The chemistry between us.

I grip his face as I stare into his eyes, studying him, memorizing him.

Fuck this, I'm moving to Atlanta.

TWENTY

Ellis

NEVER SAY NO TO DANCING...

I PICK up Kiki on my way home from the brewery. And when I see her, standing there in a little white sundress with a red flower in her hair, I can't catch my breath. "You're beautiful."

She smiles, but it doesn't reach her eyes.

"What's wrong?" I ask her.

She stops before unlocking the doors of my rental. "I'm doing a dog wedding for Yasmin, and I'd really like for you to be there."

I don't say anything, just open her car door and let her slip inside. This has my father written all over it.

He doesn't care if the dogs get married to each other. Hell, he doesn't care what happens to those dogs. Just as long as I show up at his house and he can have my ear all night long telling me how I'll never live up to his standards.

I slide into the driver's side, starting up the car. This is one wedding I want no part of, but as I look over at Kiki, I can tell this is important to her. And now it's important to me too. "Sure, I'll be there."

Her face lights up, and my breath hitches. "Thank you." She's quiet a moment before she turns to face me, resting her head against the soft leather seat. "You know where we should go?" She smiles, obviously trying to lighten the mood and I appreciate her for that. In fact, I kind of love that she did that.

"Anywhere you want."

"Anywhere?" She raises a brow.

"Uh oh, what am I getting myself into?"

"Just head downtown. We're going dancing."

Perfect, I'm a great dancer. I know many guys claim to be a great dancer, but seriously I can bust a move like no other. I steer the car onto I-95, excited to watch Kiki shake her ass all night long. Just the thought of rubbing against her on the dance floor has my cock twitching in my pants.

We pull up to the club, and it's already hopping with party-goers. Kiki's beyond excited, and I smile as we get out of the car. Relieving stress is just what I need.

She bounces a bit as we step inside. "I love dancing." Her energy is infectious.

The beat is constant, loudly vibrating throughout the dark club. Sweaty bodies line the floor, and I'm having a hard time seeing which direction we should head in. Pink, blue, orange, and every other color of lights flash over the big space, blinding me as we move through the crowd, making me hesitant.

But not Kiki, she grabs my hand and leads me straight to the dance floor. This girl is on a mission.

And it's to shake her ass. Which I'm all on board for.

"I'll get us some drinks," I say into her ear.

She gives me a thumb up with a nod and I seek out the bar.

It's not overly packed when I call out two beers easily to the bartender.

When I head back in Kiki's direction, I set the beers on the closest table and rush over to her. "Are you ok?" I ask her.

She spins around. "I'm dancing."

"I thought you were having a stroke or something." I grin...wide and take a step back. I can't even explain into words the exact things Kiki does with her body. Quick, jerky movements erupt throughout all the limbs of her body as her torso bends back and forth.

It's quite the scene here, and I laugh a little. This woman can't sing, and she definitely can't dance, but I find myself falling for her all the same.

I try to join in but stay a few feet back as not to be hit by her flailing arms.

"Isn't this fun?" she yells over the music. "You need to let loose."

"Oh, I can let loose just fine." I bust some of my killer cool dance moves that make all the women go wild. I feel the beat rushing through my veins, running down my spine. I look awesome, I'm sure.

"Are you ok?" Kiki asks me, after tapping my arm.

I pop open my eyes, leaning closer to her ear. "I'm dancing."

She raises a brow. "I don't know what that was that you were doing. You look like a robot."

"Robot?" I laugh. "Well, you look like a flailing monkey."

Her eyes grow serious and her mouth turns into a small 'o'. "I do not. I dance *amazing*."

"Right. Sure, you do." I do the 'reach back, grab my ankle and pump' dance move. Wish I knew the name of it, but I don't.

And Kiki laughs. "Oh yeah, let me show you what I got. Watch." She does some more jerky movements, looking like one of the air dancers they have on used car lots.

"That's not dancing. Watch me." I proceed to bust a move, tucking my leg into my other so I can do a cool move I've seen once in some rap video years ago. I used to practice for days until I had it perfected.

Kiki laughs, and we both gather the attention of a few other people at the club. Listen, I'm not gonna say we're the best dancers out here tonight, but we're definitely better than the older couple down by the stage, rocking back and forth.

I move my arms back and forth, lifting my leg and turning my body in a circle, letting the beat carry my body into different movements. Kiki bounces around me, and I grab a hold of her hand.

"You're a natural," I tell her over my laughter.

We work the room together, doing some sort of salsa or tango dance move, and seriously we should probably take our dance number out on the road. I think we're both great.

Hey, at least I can sing.

After a few more songs, we meld into each other's arms, rocking back and forth, not caring if we're moving too slowly for the fast beat that pumps through our bones.

I sniff her hair, letting the smell of coconuts and moonlight make me dizzy. And it does, it makes me think back to the first moment I met her, to the first moment I kissed her.

I gaze down at her, a smile on her fuckable lips, her hair a bit unruly from bouncing around earlier, and a soft glow of happiness on her face.

"Let's get out of here," I whisper to her, and she nods.

We wave to the crowd as we leave, laughing as we head out of the club. It was the dance moves making us so popular. I'm sure of it.

We rush to her house, unable to contain the next step we both want so badly.

She unlocks her front door, and already I'm thinking of all the things I want to do to her.

Before she can even shut the door, my mouth is on hers, kissing her like it's the end of the world. And if I don't get her naked right now, it might just be. My hands roam down her body, cupping her ass in my palms.

I step further inside her house, inviting myself in, like a

master of all things sexual. And tonight, I'm hoping I'm just that for her.

Trouble is, I've yet to explore every part of her. Every inch of her decadent body. Every single fiber of her being.

I peer around the room, the beige carpet underfoot, the blue couch begging me to take her there, and the way the soft moonlight pours in through the window, letting me know that sex is definitely on the menu tonight.

I grin, whispering, "I can't wait to have all of you."

Kiki closes the remaining distance between us, runs her hands down my chest, and over the bulge in my jeans. "No."

"No?" My body weeps.

"No, tonight's *my* turn."

And I am all for making it *her* turn.

She's dominating.

She's confident.

She's so goddamn sexy, that my breath hitches at the sight of her.

"Anything you want, baby." I suck, nibble, and bite along her collarbone, something I'd been thinking of doing all night.

She lets me for all of two seconds, and then she pushes on my chest once more. "No, tonight's my turn to make you feel good. Now sit," she demands, pointing to the couch.

I do as she says, because I love the little authoritative tone coming out of her pretty mouth. "Yes ma'am."

She kneels before me and oh my god, this is it. This right here is what I love. This is what gets me hard. I know right now without a shadow of a doubt; this girl owns me. Maybe she always has. Her hands fiddle with the collar of my shirt, and she undoes each button slowly, agonizingly slow, until she pulls it off. "You look so sexy."

I lean back, my body hardening when she runs her hands up my thighs. "I want these off." She tugs at the zipper of my jeans.

I help her remove them and my boxers, and she just gazes at my dick for a beat or two.

She licks her lips. "You really have a great looking dick."

I laugh a little. "Well, thank you."

Sure, I've heard it before, but having Kiki stare at it as she licks her lips makes my dick grow double size in no time.

She stands, turning on some music from her iPhone. "Hope you like this song."

"I'd like it better if you were naked, too."

And the greatest thing I've ever witnessed before in my life happens.

She's unpredictable.

She's risky.

She's sexy as fucking hell, and I can't stop eye-fucking her as she sways her hips in rhythm to the music.

Maybe this girl can't dance in a club, but in the privacy of her own home, with my lucky eyes watching her, she does a phenomenal job keeping my attention.

Fuck, I'm so damn hard.

She keeps dancing, taking off each article of clothing.

Slowly.

Daintily.

And oh, so fucking erotically. Her ass begs to me, calling me to sink my teeth into her tender flesh.

But, tonight she's in control.

Tonight, I'm at her mercy.

And oh, what a great place it is to be.

She kneels before me in nothing but her black lace panties and matching bra. "I've been wanting to do this to you for a long time." She wraps her hand around the base of my cock.

Oh fuck. My dick grows in her hand, and she licks her lips once more before bringing her mouth down on me. The moment we have contact, my hips automatically buck a little, not expecting her touch to be so smooth.

I plunge my fingers into her hair, leaning my head back as she swirls her tongue around the head of my dick. "Oh, that feels so good."

Her eyes glance up, meeting mine. And then, she closes them and sucks me further into her mouth. She's hot, and the way she's sucking on my cock makes my blood race through my system. She's got one hand on my balls, massaging them between her fingers, while her other hand rakes down my chest.

I pump the base of my cock with my fist as she works her mouth up and down my shaft. This girl's mouth is pure magic.

"I love watching you suck me into that pretty little mouth of yours," I tell her, wanting to touch her. I don't want her to stop, but at the same time I wish I was slamming my dick deep inside her.

She gets a good rhythm going, and I close my eyes, my body so close to release. I could get used to this.

Before she can even finish, I pop my dick out of her mouth. "I need to be deep inside you. I can't wait," I tell her, unable to think about anything else.

She stands, and I run my hand up the side of her leg, past her knee, up to the inside of her thigh until I hit the lace of her panties. I pull them off, and rub my fingers over her wetness, bringing my tongue down to taste her. Sweet and spicy, and I swipe my tongue over her to get another taste. Fuck.

She grinds her pussy into my face, and I let her. Oh boy, do I fucking let her. I toy my tongue around her clit, her fingers digging into my scalp as I push harder against her skin.

"You're already so wet for me." I gaze up at her, positioning her to get on her hands and knees on the couch as I move in behind her.

She's so soft and smooth. Everything about her is tight and hot. Even her fucking mouth sucking on my cock was sweltering. I'm so turned on, even the mere thought of fucking Kiki from behind gets my cock ready to explode.

I slap her right ass cheek, grabbing a hold of it and squeezing afterwards. "I've been thinking about fucking you like this all night."

She peeks over her shoulder, biting her lower lip. "Do it."

I run the tip of my cock over her tight center. "Is this what you want?"

She nods, and I lean my head toward hers to kiss her.

I push my dick inside her, stopping when I'm all the way in and just continue kissing her. I trace my fingers over her slender neck, and dip my tongue deeper into her mouth. "I love kissing you," I tell her when I break away.

Her big brown eyes watch me as I rock my dick in and out of her. And it feels so fucking good. I keep thrusting in and out and in and out, again and again, squeezing her neck slightly. My other hand controls her hip, my fingers digging into her soft flesh.

I bite my lower lip as I dive deeper into her. I'm so hard, harder than I've ever been as I keep pushing and pushing, screwing and fucking her until all I can hear are her moans echoing throughout the room.

And it eggs me on, making me go even faster, trying my best to get her to scream. And then she does, letting loose and throwing her head back. "Ellis," she calls out, "I'm so close."

It's like she's said the right words. The words that make my body snap into motion even faster, trying my best to not come just yet. I can't get over how tight she is. How perfect her little ass is as I grip my palm around it. How sexy she sounds when she calls out my name like she can't get enough either.

"I'll do anything you want, Kiki." I drive in deeper. "Anything. Your sexual fantasies are my desire to fulfill."

"Anything?"

"Yeah, baby." I shove my cock all the way inside her, and still my movements.

Her body keeps rocking. "Don't stop."

"What do you want from me?"

"I want to come all over your dick, and then taste your come."

Oh, shit. Fuck. I pull her hair, bringing her head back to me. "Come all over me, you're so fucking ready." I start my movements again, striking, pushing, and fucking this girl with all I have.

Her orgasm begins low, her moans barely audible, and builds to something amazing. She cries out, "I'm coming." And she rides me, slapping her body against mine.

And as soon as she's done, she moves away to kneel before me. My dick pulsing, missing her tight cunt to slam into.

She opens her mouth and I swear I've died and gone to heaven. I pump my dick in my fist, grunting, groaning, pushing my cock against her tongue.

And then it all comes to a yielding halt, my orgasm shooting through me like a rocket. "Take my come deep down your throat."

There's never been a better sight than Kiki right here and right now. How could I ever leave this?

TWENTY-ONE

Kiki

NEVER TRUST YOUR MOTHER...

IT'S BEEN A VERY frantic week with Ellis and me. We've been trying new flavors of girly beer, as he likes to call it, and we finally came up with a wheat beer with strawberries that he thinks will knock the pink socks off women everywhere.

And I agree.

Today after work Ellis is bringing me along to hit a restaurant to see if they'll want to carry his beer. I told him I didn't feel right coming along, but he said he wanted to see me and spend time with me.

It's sweet.

He picks me up, and we head off down the road to a little bar called Dune Dog Cafe. I've driven by the place a few times, but have never been inside. It's always packed, and if Ellis can get them to carry his beer it would be huge for them.

We pull into the small parking area, and Ellis and I walk in together. This isn't like we're a couple having dinner, no this is business and I try to keep my demeanor serious so as not to ruin any chances with Ellis and the owner.

The owner greets us, and introduces himself as Dave. He's very laid-back, and I relax a little. He pulls us off to a small table near the back and asks if we want a drink.

Ellis holds up the cooler he's carrying and says, "I have plenty here."

Dave laughs. "Now that's what I like to hear." He sits down. "Let's try some of this beer you have."

I scan the small bar, it's very beachy, and all outdoors. Almost like you're at one of the pavilions down by the shore. The breeze sweeps through the restaurant, making it the perfect setting for a nice meal.

Ellis opens the cooler, pulling out the first beer he's brought along. The pale ale called Luau that I love so much. Ellis pops the top and hands it to Dave.

Dave takes a nice hefty gulp, and then sets the bottle down. "Damn, that's really good and fruity."

I smile, happy that he's liking it. And I sit back, in awe of how Ellis sells to this man. The confidence. The sexy conviction he exudes.

"Now, try this one. I think you'll appreciate the smoothness of it." He pops open the Twist & Stout, handing it over to him, and then giving me a little wink.

Dave takes a longer drink this time, letting the full flavors of the hops explode in his mouth. "Ok. This one's a winner. I have to have this one."

Ellis laughs. "Ok, ok. Absolutely we can get this one for you. I can do three-fifty for a half barrel. Or if you order three I can drop that down to three-twenty."

Dave nods. "I like that price. I'll buy the one. I don't sell that much stout."

"I want to show you another beer we've been working on and then we can discuss prices for all the different types of beer we offer." Ellis digs into his cooler, pulling out the pink bottle with the swirly designs. "Now this is a hefeweizen geared toward women with strawberry flavors."

Dave holds the bottle in his hands, studying it before taking a sip. "Wow, that's a good wheat beer." He smiles. "This is a pretty damn good idea. I have tons of women who would drink this shit up."

Ellis laughs, getting along with the owner of this small little wooden place so well. "Let's go over some numbers."

My phone dings in my pocket and I glance at the screen. "I'll be right back, I just need to take this." I excuse myself, and once I'm far enough away I answer Poppi's call.

She just wants to tell me the accounting paperwork she misplaced last week has been found. I step outside of the Dune Dog Cafe and run smack dab into my mother.

I end the call with Poppi. "Mom, what are you doing here?" I give her a hug, nodding toward my Aunt Carol.

"We're having dinner. You should join us," my mother says.

"I'm so sorry to hear about Henry." My aunt Carol squeezes me extra tight.

"It's ok," I peer over my shoulder at Ellis and Dave, "I'm fine."

"Come sit with us," my mother nods over my shoulder, "there'll be three of us for dinner," she tells the hostess.

"Mom, I uhh…" Shoot. Ellis and Dave are walking this way.

Dave smiles, like the good owner of a bar would. "Thank you for coming in," he shakes my hand, patting the other hand on Ellis' back, "dinner's on me."

Both my aunt's and my mother's mouths drop just a bit as they scan their eyes over Ellis and Dave.

"Thank you, Dave. We'll talk soon."

Dave waves and walks away, leaving me with my mother and my aunt and... Ellis.

"I don't believe we've met," Ellis says, shaking my mother's hand and then my aunt's. "I'm Ellis Atwood."

"Do you work here?" my mother asks.

He laughs a little. "No. I own the Bearded Goat Brewery."

"I love that beer," Aunt Carol pipes in. "Will you be joining us too?"

I shrug. "Sure, why not." I introduce Ellis and as soon as he hears it's my mother he grins even harder.

This isn't how I would normally bring a man home to meet my mother, but it works.

"I've always loved it here," Aunt Carol says, pointing at the decor. "The colorful surfboards everywhere are so lively."

"I know. That's why I recommended we come here," my mother says with a laugh. "Kiki, what were you doing here?"

We all sit down at a picnic table, and pick up the menus already waiting for us. Ellis pushes the cooler he's carrying under his seat and smiles. "We were selling my beer, trying our best to become a vendor here."

My mother raises a brow. "And you needed Kiki for that? I'm confused, Kiki, did you get a job at the brewery?"

"Well, Ms..."

"Call me, Lisa," my mother says.

"...Lisa. Kiki and I are kind of ..." he doesn't finish his thought because we actually haven't had 'the talk'. You know the one, the what-exactly-are-we-doing-here talk. I mean we spend so much time together, and we've had loads of sex, and I swear I'm connecting to this man more than I've ever connected with anyone, but without the actual talk neither of us wants to assume anything.

"We're kind of seeing each other, Mom," I pipe in, helping Ellis out.

He smiles wide, throwing his arm around my shoulder,

sending chills straight down my spine. "And Kiki has been instrumental in keeping my brewery afloat."

He's just talking me up here. I haven't been instru-anything.

Both my mother's and Aunt Carol's eyebrows raise in unison. "Really? Is this true?"

"I haven't been *that* instrumental. Ellis is just being nice."

Ellis runs a finger over his bottom lip as he watches my mother and Aunt interrogate me about the brewery. Then, he grabs the cooler under his seat. "She was the mastermind behind this." He produces two bottles of the pink beer.

My mother grabs it like it's an alien head, and studies the bottle, and then sets it back down. "What is it?"

"It's a beer geared toward women. It's a strawberry hefeweizen, try it." He pops both tops, handing them out.

Aunt Carol is the first to respond. "Wow, this is nice. Smooth."

My mother, more skeptical, takes a tentative sip. "Oh, this *is* good. And Kiki," she faces me now, "you thought of this?"

I give a little shrug. "Yeah, well I like beer."

"And now you're dating Ellis?"

I smile, with another shrug. "Yeah, I am." But don't ask me where it's going because we haven't even worked out the details with each other.

My mother smiles. "How did the two of you meet?"

"Yes, we want all the details," Aunt Carol chimes in, taking another sip of her beer.

Umm. Where do I even begin? Ellis and I exchange a weird look, both of us probably thinking the same thing. How do we even tell our story?

"Well, I saw her, liked her, and kissed her." Ellis laughs, and my mother and Aunt Carol laugh along as well, not really understanding the whole joke, obviously.

"Mom, it's a long story. But, we're happy. And I know now I never loved Henry."

My mother tears up. "I'm so happy for you two."

Aunt Carol launches in about her own daughter's wedding, telling Ellis about every single detail of it. "And we have peacocks," she says, continuing on with her story.

My mother nods at me. "Let's use the restroom."

I feel a bit bad about leaving Ellis alone with my aunt while she brags about Marsha, Marsha, Marsha, but it's obvious my mother has something to say.

I kiss Ellis' cheek before I leave.

We excuse ourselves and head in the direction of the restrooms. In the hallway, my mother stops and turns to face me. Her brown eyes searching mine.

"I know I've been hard on you…"

"What?" I cut in.

She waves her hand, to let her finish. "No, I've been so consumed with Carol and Marsha that I never really asked you what *you* wanted."

"Oh, Mom, it's ok."

She isn't finished. "I was a monster," I laugh a little, "and I never should have put that kind of pressure on you." She hugs me, tight and true.

"I'm fine."

"I can see that now. There's this bright glow all around you, and I can see it in your eyes when you look at Ellis." She smiles, swiping a tear off her own cheek. "You never loved Henry, and I can see that now."

I hug her again. "Mom, I really like this one," speaking about Ellis.

And I really appreciate my mother saying this to me. For too long I've felt the pressure of Marsha's life affecting my own. Many times, I've felt I couldn't live up to the expectations set on me. It's like a big weight has been lifted and I smile.

"Mom, thank you," I tell her.

She glances back at Ellis. "I can tell he really likes you, too."

LATER THAT NIGHT, when I'm tucked neatly into the side of Ellis, which I'm realizing is one of my most favorite places to be, I sigh with happiness. I could really get used to this. I want to bring up Atlanta. I want to bring up all the things of the unknown, and get answers.

But, instead I pop my head up. "Are you sleeping?"

"Well, not now." He laughs, and I know he wasn't sleeping. I hope.

"I'm just wondering when you'll hear from Henry about getting the money to start producing the dog beer and other stuff?" I smile. "And I want you to know I'll be ordering some of the dog beer for my shop."

He runs his fingers through my hair when I lay my head back on his chest. "Thank you." He kisses the top of my head. "Urban says Henry's been kind of flighty. Like when we call, no answer. So, Urban invited him to Yasmin's wedding. He props up on an elbow. "I hope that's ok."

I nod, hoping the reason Henry's not answering doesn't have to do with Ellis and me. "Sure." I twirl my finger over the six-pack abs he's got on him. "Are you mad I'm making you go?"

He laughs lightly, his chest moving up and down. "No, it'll be ok. This is important to you. So, it makes it important to me too."

"I just know how much you dislike your father."

He shakes his head. "I was in high school when my father cheated on my mother." He shakes his head, most likely remembering it all. "How can a man do that to the woman he loves?"

"I don't know."

"He left my mother with nothing. Absolutely nothing, and she was the one who stood by him and he ruined everything by leaving."

"I'm so sorry."

"From that point my father became worse. He became very

showboaty about his life, and all his belongings. Then, he started gambling and it has just snowballed from there."

"I understand." We lay in silence for a moment as Ellis continues running his fingers through my hair. "Is your mom better now?"

"Yeah, she actually lives up in Atlanta down the street from me."

"And she's happy?"

He kisses the top of my head. "Yeah, she's happy. And like I said. This wedding is important to you, so I'll be there to support you and only you."

This man makes me feel all mushy inside. I lean up, pressing a kiss against his abdominals. "Thank you."

He hisses when I make contact with his skin, and then he sits up. "I'm serious. This is who you are. You're a dog wedding planner, and I love that about you."

My ears perk up at the mention of love. "I love that you're a beer guy."

He cracks a smile. "I'm a little bit more than that. You forgot kickass dancer, awesome beer master, graphic designs that will knock your socks off."

I laugh. "And you forgot about the bedroom."

"Oh, right. I'm an ok lover." He grins wide.

I kiss his cheek. "You're so much better than just ok."

He kisses me quick on the lips. "It's because of you. It's easy with you."

"I hope that's a compliment."

He shakes his head. "That's not what I meant. I just mean, it's like we're always on the same page. It's a great feeling."

"They say dogs have an internal connection to their owners. That when they're sad, the dog is sad and so on. I feel like we kind of have the same connection."

Ellis breathes in my hair, smothering his face in the soft curls before pulling back. "I like that." And then he kisses me, long and slow, smooth and deep, his tongue penetrating me to the point of complete arousal. When he finishes, he pulls back, cupping my cheeks in both hands. "I really like that."

I kiss him, because if I don't I might end up blurting out words like love, marriage, and forever. And even though we have this amazing link between us, I don't want to rush things.

TWENTY-TWO

Ellis

NEVER COUNT your eggs before they hatch...

I THINK I could watch Kiki sleep all day long. Is that creepy? That's creepy, right? Well, I mean it in a she's just so fucking cute kind of way. And she is, seriously.

I kiss her cheek and crawl out of bed, padding my way into the kitchen to start a pot of coffee. Yesterday after we left Dune Dog's my phone had two missed calls from two more places that wanted to carry our beer. Dave raved about it, and I plan on telling Urban the good news. Once we get the money from the investors and sign the contract, life should be great for the Bearded Goat Brewery.

My whole world is looking up.

I let the coffee percolate, and the smell travels throughout Kiki's cute little cottage. She lucked out in finding this place. It's close to the beach, on a quiet little road, with not that many neighbors.

I get the cream ready, and make myself a mug and take it outside to sit on her patio. The weather is cool this early in the morning, and I relax as I try to come up with a game plan for today.

"Heard about Dune Dog's, that's awesome," Urban texts me.

I throw back another. "Two more places just called and I plan on checking them out."

"Perfect. Dad's wondering if you can stop by his place. Noon." I read Urban's text, wondering what my father could possibly have to say to me. A ball of nerves churns deep inside my belly. This can't be good.

I finish my coffee, making my way back into the kitchen to rinse the mug.

"Morning sleepyhead," I say when I spot Kiki making her way into the room, her eyes still sleepy and her hair a mess. She looks cuter than I've ever seen her.

"Coffee," she mumbles.

Ah, my girl is not a morning person. I pull down a mug and pour her some piping hot coffee.

She breathes it in. "What are you doing up so early on a Saturday?"

"Work, baby. Always work." I smile and kiss her cheek. "Actually, I have to meet Urban at my father's house. He has something to talk to us about." My smile turns tight and I can't help rolling my eyes a bit.

"Uh oh. I hope it's ok."

"I'm sure it will be." I wrap my arms around her. "And what's on your agenda today?"

"I have to pick up a few things for Yasmin's wedding."

"Dinner after?"

"Absolutely." We're falling into this perfect little rhythm and I fucking love it.

I PULL into my father's mansion by the water, and spot Urban's SUV. Thank god he's here before me.

The house on the hill boasts wealth, importance, and a lie he's trying desperately to hold on to. It has all the elements of things to compete with all the neighbors. A grand yard, big columns, and a dock with a boat tied off to the end of it.

I really don't want to be here. But, I'll play the game. Whatever game that is. My father looks at life like a game of chess. He positions the pieces so that no matter which move you make he's already calling checkmate before you even know what's happened.

But not this time, not today.

"Ellis, so glad you're here," my father says with a tight smile.

"What do you need to see us for?" I ask him before I've even completely stepped into his house.

Of course, my father is one of *those* types. He needs to set the mood, have us come inside. Light cigars. Drink our tea. Act like civilized folk, and all that other horseshit.

Urban obliges, stepping inside and making small talk until my father has us sitting inside his office. It's a power play.

Him sitting there behind his big cherry-wood desk, degrees from the various universities he graduated from decorating the wall behind him, and us in the chairs on the opposite side. He towers over everything in the room even in a seated position, like his chair is on the highest setting. Another power move.

Hell, all he's missing is the red tie to show he means business.

But, not today. He wears a Tommy Bahama shirt, blue with a white hibiscus flower pattern. He pulls out a little wooden box from his humidifier case. Ah, the cigars.

I decline, but Urban and my father light theirs up.

"Are we about done with all the theatrics?" I lean back in my stiff wooden chair, trying my best not to look as displeased as I feel. But, that's easier said than done.

"Ellis, you should be grateful I don't throw you off this new project you and that girl have started." My father stares at me from behind his dark-rimmed glasses.

"Don't threaten me, old man." Ha. I'd like to see Daddy dearest try.

He holds up his hands in surrender. "Ok, we're getting off on the wrong foot here. I called you both over because I feel like you'll need me to move forward."

"Need you?" I ask, and before I can go any further Urban stands from his chair.

"Dad, while we appreciate the help, I think Ellis and I can take it from here. We're seconds away from closing the deal with Henry, and have all the products ready for production."

"Yes, but we need a face for the new products, and I think that's where I need to take the reins. I need to showcase my new products to the world."

"Ah, so you get the credit."

"Well, it is *my* brewery," my father says, his eyes gleaming with dollar signs. Wonder how long it will take him to gamble away the future earnings.

"No deal." I rest my hand on his desk. "I'm not here helping so you can just get us into the same predicament next year."

Urban sits back in his chair. "He's right, Dad. We can't have things getting as bad as before."

My father hangs his head for just a moment, really for show more than anything else. "You're right, boys. I need to be better. I will be better," says any good junkie who needs his next fix, and for my father it's gambling.

"Ok, seriously. If we need to get you into some sort of rehab, we will," Urban says.

My father laughs. "I'll be good."

Richard Atwood could never be seen at a rehabilitation center for gamblers, or for anything else for that matter. The country club gossip would fly through the roof, and they'd not be invited to their weekly squash game.

I stare at my father, the anger I've had toward him doubling over, begging to be released. "I'll believe it when I see it."

My father sits up straight, puffing out his chest. "Urban, give us a minute."

Urban nods, leaving the room.

Richard Atwood doesn't speak right away, instead he studies me over his glasses, puffing on his cigar. "You really hate me, don't you?" he finally asks, his voice low and concise.

"I really do."

"You know your mother has forgiven me for what happened all those years ago."

I laugh. "No, she just doesn't care about you."

"Ellis, do you know what the opposite of love is?"

"Hate." Because everything coursing through my bones is the opposite of love right now.

He shakes his head, like he knows everything in the world. His smugness nearly kills me. "No, it's indifference. When you no longer care, and all the anger melts away. That's when you know you no longer love someone."

"That's what happened with Mom? You left her because you didn't care?"

My father shakes his head. "No, you're missing my point." He stands, moving over to look out the window. "What happened between your mother and me was all my fault. And I've felt worthless for many years because of it."

"Good."

He snaps back to stare in my direction. "Sometimes you don't realize you're making the wrong choices until it's too late." He hangs his head low, hands joined behind his back. "And then you're left with a lifetime of regret."

I stand. "Thanks for the life lesson, *Dad*."

I walk out of his office, not looking back.

TWENTY-THREE

Kiki

NEVER TRUST AN EX...

"JUST HOLD STILL TITAN," I say to the little maltipoo sitting on the leather chair next to his owner, a very relaxed Mrs. Gold. "You'll love this, promise." I start his blueberry facial, rubbing the mixture over his smooth coat of fur.

"He always smells so yummy after we leave here," Mrs. Gold says, enjoying her very own blueberry facial I finished moments earlier.

I keep rubbing, making sure his fur is fully covered, and then move him over to the small sink to rinse.

"All done," I say when I finish rinsing out the product. "Marge will be in to finish you both up."

Marge's job is to dry and comb the pups, and then gets them all ready for the mani/pawdi they'll be having.

My mind thinks back to when Ellis was sitting in this very

room, my hands running over his smooth face. Chills erupt at the thought of the way he stared at me with all the intensity in the world.

I wash my hands, and then make my way back out to the front entrance to wait for my next client.

"What do you think of this?" Poppi asks, holding out a magazine of the newest bachelor and how the girl who won the whole show and got the rose and engagement broke up.

"Can't say I didn't see that coming," I say with a laugh.

Before Poppi can say anything more, Henry walks inside like he owns the place, carrying a little white poodle with him. A brunette scurries behind him, her gray eyes fixed on Henry. She looks familiar and I realize it's the bartender from Bearded Goat.

"Hi Kiki, this is Mia." Then he holds up the little poodle. "And this is Alaska."

I smile. "Great name for a great dog." And then I reach my hand out to shake Mia's. "Hi, nice to meet you."

Henry throws an arm around Mia's shoulders. "She's my fiancée."

And there it is, all shiny on her left ring finger, the same rock that Henry proposed to me with. The very ring that travelled through little Peter the goat's digestive tract.

Wonder how many other places it's gone.

"Oh, wow." I glance wide-eyed at Poppi before congratulating the happy couple. "Congratulations. How can I help you today?"

"We're here to get Alaska and Mia the Spawsome whatever thing." Henry waves his hand as if he can't be bothered to read the package names. But then again, he's always been like this.

Not really paying attention.

Never really reading into any type of situation.

How had I never noticed it before?

And now it all clicks. He was never in love with me. He's in love with being made partner at his big fancy firm.

I smile, like the professional I am, and tap a few keys on the computer, checking the schedule. "I have an opening right now, actually." Thank goodness Miss Mingle canceled. "Poppi can take you in the back." I wave my hand, pointing to the set of white French doors and Poppi hops into action.

"Absolutely, follow me." Poppi pushes the doors open and Mia follows behind with Alaska in hand.

"How are you?" Henry asks as soon as we're alone.

"I'm good. Listen, Henry," I need to tell him, "I'm kind of seeing Ellis now."

Henry laughs like this news could ever be true. "I know. It's not that I have you followed or anything."

"Oh, ok. I just wanted you to know."

He smiles down his nose at me. "I always am in the know, Kiki."

What's that supposed to mean?

"It means Kiki. Ellis needs me. He doesn't need some dog shop owner like you." He steps closer, smoothing out the non-existent wrinkles in his tailor-made suit. "It means I'm keeping the brewery going. I'm the one who's going to keep all the little stupid ideas you have of dog beer and pink beer," he rolls his eyes, "afloat."

I blink, not really sure of the reaction he's looking for from me.

"You're grateful I'm doing this for them, right?"

I nod. "Yes."

"I could very easily get the firm to pull the deal like," he snaps his fingers, "that."

"Don't do that. Please, Henry. I know things didn't work out between us, but the brewery deserves a chance."

Henry laughs. "There's one thing you need to know about me, Kiki."

"What's that?"

He puffs out his chest. "I'm a winner. Always have been, always will be."

"What does that have to do with anything?"

He steps close, almost too close, and I'm thankful for the counter keeping us apart. "I always win."

"Ok."

"And for me to invest in the brewery and save the day I need something from you."

"Me?"

"Yes you."

I don't like the sound of this. At all. And I'm afraid to even ask what he needs me to do.

But, I don't need to because Henry tells me, like he's all too excited to get the words out, "I want you to break up with Ellis." There's a gleam in his eyes, and I know he's loving this request.

I'm dumbfounded. "How could you even ask that of me?" My face scrunches up with anger. I wish I could ask this ass to leave, but he's a paying customer, so I tap away at the computer. "That'll be sixty-five thirty."

He pulls out his wallet, handing over his credit card. "I'm serious here, Kiki. I can't work with a company where the owner is fucking my ex."

"Please leave." I don't care if this goes against my own company standards. I wrote the handbook, so I'm allowed to break them.

"Kiki, do you want to see the Atwood's lose everything they have?"

I don't move a muscle. "Well, no."

"Exactly. Now, how serious is this little puppy dog crush you have on each other anyway?"

I don't want to tell Henry that I think I'm falling for Ellis, and that I think Ellis may be feeling the same way, so I keep my mouth clamped shut.

"Let me tell you something about Ellis. He's not serious about you." Henry laughs. "He's just using you. Do you think a man like Ellis would ever go for someone like you?"

Ouch. "You did," I spit out, holding my chin up.

NEVER KISS A STRANGER

Henry doesn't say a word, just pushes off the counter, checking his watch before staring out the glass door that leads to the street. He watches the cars pass by for a moment before turning to face me once more. "I'm serious here, Kiki. I don't lose. The only ones who are going to lose from your selfishness are the Atwood's." He pushes open the door, glancing over his shoulder. "I expect you to do the right thing." And then he walks through the door, pushing his sunglasses over his eyes, not even looking back. I definitely won't be here when he comes to pick up the dog and his soon-to-be-bride, that's for sure.

⊏⊐

I'VE BEEN in a sour mood for days since Henry left my shop and told me to break up with Ellis. I've been over and over it again in my head. I can't break up with him. I really *really* like him times a thousand more reallys. I also don't want him and his family to lose the brewery.

This is a moment for ice cream. Mint chocolate chip to be exact.

But, no. This problem is so much more serious than ice cream can handle. And besides, I can't pop open a tub right here where I am.

Ugh, I wish I had someone to talk to about this. Lola and Poppi would just tell me to say 'no' to Henry and ride off into the sunset with Ellis.

It's not that easy. In fact, it's the most complicated shit on the planet. Like I would need a nuclear physicist to try to figure it all out. And still, I don't think he could even come close.

I care about Ellis. I do. And I can't let him lose the funding for his projects. I can't let them lose everything if the brewery doesn't make it.

But, I also don't want to rush into things. I made that mistake with Henry, and look where that got me. Ellis lives in Atlanta. I live here.

"Do you have the flowers, Kiki?" Poppi asks when she finds me gazing out over the water. We're here at the Atwood's home on the Intracoastal, and trying desperately to get all the prep work done for Doodles and Sparkles wedding.

"Is it weird the bride and groom are brother and sister?" I ask Poppi, handing her the bouquet of flowers.

She laughs. "Is it weirder they have more people attending their wedding than I'll ever have at my own."

I continue stringing the lights, making this another spectacular wedding. I need to make sure I get lots of pictures for the portfolio. "Yeah," I say, absentmindedly.

"You're awfully quiet." Poppi stops working. "Want to talk about it?"

I slump my shoulders in defeat, desperate to get a little advice. "If you had the ability to save someone's future, would you?"

Poppi studies me for a moment before answering, "Is this about the brewery?"

I nod.

"What's going on exactly?"

I probably shouldn't tell her, and even saying it out loud is a bit ridiculous, but I do it anyway. "Henry won't help the brewery unless I break up with Ellis."

"Oh, wow," she says while blowing out a deep breath. "I always knew that man was a…" she doesn't say whatever profanity she's thinking of for Henry, and so many would fit so well.

"I know."

"Are you honestly thinking about doing it?" She places the string of lights down on a nearby table, then rests both hands on my shoulder, looking me directly in the eyes. "You can't let that man control you."

"But Ellis' life is in Atlanta and mine is here."

Poppi shrugs. "So?"

"So…it'll never work out."

"Never say never," she says. "Sounds to me you've already decided, and not giving the unknown a chance." She drops her hands, picking up the lights again. "Sometimes we make rash decisions because we're not sure of the outcome."

"I can't be the reason their brewery fails." I've made up my mind. And not because I'm afraid to think about how Ellis and I would work as a couple with him in Atlanta and me here. But because I can't let him lose everything. And this is bigger than just Ellis. There's a whole company to think of. Urban, all the employees, everything.

I can't be the sole reason everyone is out of a job.

With my mood worsening by the minute, I continue the setup of the back yard.

"This is all so beautiful," Yasmin says. "You've done a wonderful job transforming this place." She studies the string of lights we're setting up. "This will all be so perfect."

"It's coming together nicely." Geeze, I can't even fake being pleasant. It's like all the good mood has been sucked dry from my being, and I'm left with this emptiness inside.

Yasmin pictured an evening wedding, with soft twinkling lights over head as the two pups bark their vows to each other. The yard is littered with white fold-out chairs, an aisle made of white tulle, and a bride dressed to the nines in one of the prettiest little wedding dresses I've ever seen.

"Sparkles looks amazing," I tell Yasmin as Poppi finishes the last strand of lights. "Just an hour to go until guests start arriving." And I have to check on the food. "Excuse me." I head off toward the kitchen.

Ellis pops a pig in a blanket into his mouth as I walk in. "You do know this is all ridiculous right?"

"What is? My job?"

He cocks a brow. "No, the fact they can spend money on this but can't pay my old man's gambling debts."

My heart breaks a little for Ellis. "I know. I'm so sorry."

He shrugs, looking delectable in his black button-down shirt and black jeans. "What can you do, right?" He's so upbeat it should be illegal.

"Yeah." Although I know what I can do. I can make sure Ellis gets the money Henry delivers so they can save the brewery. "I just need to check on a few things." I rush out of the kitchen before I tell Ellis everything I'm planning.

I know, it's all sorts of fucked up in a world of madness. Why can't life just be easy?

Ha. Of course, that can never happen. I finally find someone I could possibly spend the rest of my life with and this happens. Don't dwell on what ifs, I tell myself.

As soon as I step out of the kitchen I run smack dab into a brick wall. "Oh, Henry," I say, stepping back and fixing my hair. "I didn't see you there."

"Kiki, I was just stopping by to see how our little arrangement was going." He smirks this devil-like smile, and I so wish I could slap it off his face.

I don't want to tell him he's won, but he has.

I'd do anything for Ellis.

TWENTY-FOUR

Ellis

NEVER STOP CHASING...

SHOULD I be happy two dogs are getting married? Normally, sure. I love a good dog wedding just like the next guy. But today, my mood is all over the place.

I can't believe my father, throwing this lavish party for all his socialite friends and their socialite pups. This place looks like a poodle stomping ground. I don't think I've ever seen so many poodles with pink bows in their hair in all my life.

Come on, I know I haven't.

This isn't my scene.

Back home in Atlanta, I'm just a normal guy. I don't entertain. And I definitely don't dress my dog up, if I had one.

And after meeting Kiki I really want one. There's a lot I realize my life was missing before. Since meeting her, I've realized I'd been leading an empty, meaningless life.

The guests arrive, and I take my seat next to Henry. He's a bit cockier today if you can believe that. Like he's in on a little secret that I'm not privy to. Hope it's about money. "You got those projection figures I emailed over last night, right?" I whisper to him before the ceremony takes place.

He nods. "Perfect. I love it all."

I swell with pride, knowing all my hard work and well, Kiki's grand ideas, will all soon be coming to fruition.

Yasmin calls for Sparkles, and the dog trots down the aisle. I may have rolled my eyes when Sparkles sits perfectly at the dais like she does this every day. Who knows, I could see Yasmin doing this daily with her dogs.

The whole crowd ooh's and ahh's when they're pronounced husband and wife by Kiki. Even though I can't get behind this particular dog wedding, I can definitely get behind Kiki. Get your mind out of the gutter. But, I'd do that too.

She's got a brain wealthy of ideas, and I'm the lucky son-of-a-bitch she shares them with. I'm the lucky man who gets to be close to all her genius. All her pure awesomeness. Seriously, she's life-changing.

I've been thinking a lot. And I'm ready to uproot my whole life to be with this woman. As I sit here and watch her, long brown hair flowing in the breeze, her blue strappy dress accentuating every sexy curve I know she has, and a smile to light up the whole enchanted evening. This girl is like ice cream on a gloomy day. Mint chocolate chip, to be exact.

I've never been in love, but this is damn near the closest I've ever been to it. And staring at her right now as she tries to help two dogs back down the aisle, I realize I've already fallen so hard for her there's no escaping it.

She touches my shoulder as she passes down the aisle and it sends a shockwave straight through me. And without a shadow of a doubt, I know I want this whole thing with her. Life. Love. Marriage. Hell, even a happily ever after.

AFTER PARTIES for weddings are sick. Now imagine that times ten. Yes, for a dog wedding. Like this is insanity, and my father's whole back yard has been turned into a nightclub with flashing strobe lights and a dancefloor.

Urban and Henry involve me in a conversation for most of the night as I keep catching glances of Kiki every time she passes by.

And I swear she takes my breath away each time she smiles. I wonder if that feeling of eagles swarming in my chest will ever go away when I look at her.

Her and her friends are busily keeping food stocked, and drinks full, and I just want to grab her hand and take her back to my hotel more than anything in the world.

But, I play the game.

I socialize with Henry because we need his firm. Laughing at all his pompous jokes. His snide remarks. Man, this guy really is an ass.

How had I never noticed before?

I tell a few people about the dog beer we'll be launching in just a few short months. The amount of interest is insane, and I'm excited to tell Kiki.

A while later, I find myself standing alone, overlooking the party like a bystander not wanting to get too close.

"Great party, isn't it?" my father asks, stepping up beside me. He looks out over the water, holding his cigar away from his mouth. "Want one?" He holds out another in his hand, and I take it from his hand.

"Great party." And only because a great girl orchestrated it.

He hands me the cigar cutter, and I chop off the tip. "Let me light that for you." He produces a lighter, and I breathe in the sweet taste of oak and chestnut.

We stand quietly together, sucking on our cigars and looking out over the calm waters of the Intracoastal. There's so many things I need to say to him, but I can't muster up a single word. It's been too long. The animosity has grown into something unrecognizable, even to me.

It eats away at me, leaving nothing but sticks and bones, and I try with everything I can to pick up the pieces and work through the madness in my mind.

Is my dad a bad guy? Absolutely. But, maybe parts of me have been shut off to the idea of a healthy reunion for so many years.

Maybe he's right about hate not being the opposite of love. Maybe I'm fucking growing up, and need to put the bad blood behind me. My mother has. Why can't I?

"Kiki's a great girl," he says, breaking down a barrier to try to extend the tiniest of an olive branch my way.

"Yeah, she's definitely something else." I chuckle a little at the thought of Kiki dancing and singing.

"Hold onto a girl like her."

"Like you held onto Mom?" The daggers can no longer be contained.

"Now what happened between me and your mother was a long time ago. I've apologized, and she's forgiven me, why can't you?"

"Because you never apologized to me."

He doesn't say anything for a while, before breathing out a measly, "I never realized you expected an apology too."

"I didn't expect one, Dad," I turn to face him, "I deserve one."

He blinks at me.

"Nice party. How much did this one set you back? You know we need money for these projects, right? Maybe if you just did *something* you could be proud of in your whole fucking life." I walk away, unable to face him a second longer, the light of the moon leading my way closer to the lapping waves. I snub out the cigar and place it next to my shoes. Maybe the soft sand between my toes will help.

"I was looking for you." Kiki walks up behind me, kicking off her shoes. "Is everything ok?"

I take in a deep breath of the cool air and let it out smoothly. "Yeah, just my father." I turn to face her as she dips her toes into the water. "It's like this party for example, he can fund this but can't pay back the loan Bearded Goat gave him."

"I know."

"Like I don't know where his head's at." I glance over my shoulder at the lights of the party, not stopping anytime soon. "It's like his priorities are so twisted up."

"Have you talked to him about it?"

I stuff my hands in my pockets. "Yeah, Urban and I tried. He doesn't care."

"Well, you have Henry. So, everything will work out."

"Yeah, thank god we have Henry."

Kiki's eyes grow serious and I remove a hand from my pocket to swipe back a strand of brown hair floating across her face. I tuck it behind her ear and then continue a path down her cheek. So fucking soft.

"I need to tell you something, Ellis."

"Are you alright?"

She shakes her head, pushing my hand away from her face. "No, listen. I think you're a great person," Oh no. "but I can't do this. There's no future for us. And even if there was, I can't be with you."

This is out of nowhere. "I thought we were getting along so well."

"I'm so sorry, Ellis." And she rushes away from me, back to the party.

And don't worry, I rush right after her once I've grabbed my shoes. I'm not a fucking idiot.

The minute I get back to the party it's loud, chaotic, too many bright lights and flashing colors, and people everywhere, blocking my view. I push a stranger out of my way, apologizing under my breath as I push another. The noise level has amped up, and Kiki is nowhere to be seen. I scan the crowd, making my way through them best I can as I try to find her.

Everything had been like a dream. Was it all one-sided? I don't think so, no I know so. It's real. And Kiki feels it too.

I spot Poppi and head in her direction. "Have you seen Kiki?"

She looks lost and shakes her head. "I think she just left. Is everything ok?"

"No, it isn't." And I run away. After the woman I know for sure I've fallen for.

TWENTY-FIVE

Kiki

NEVER TRUST YOURSELF...

THAT WAS the hardest thing I've ever done. And the moment Ellis ran after me, I knew I wanted to turn around, to hug him and say I'd never leave him ever again. But I couldn't. I can't give in.

I need Henry to follow through with his end of the deal, and I text him right before I start my van, "it's done."

I drive away, not really sure where I'm going but I know I can't go home. I can't go to the Dog Spaw. I can't go anywhere Ellis may be able to find me.

I need time away. I need to heal.

I need to bawl my fucking eyes out.

Because I walked away from him once, and I don't know if I saw him if I could do it again. In fact, I know I can't.

So, I head to the one place I know I can find some peace. My mother's house.

I pull into her driveway, and all the lights are off. Ugh. I hope I don't wake her.

I creep up the cobblestone pathway leading to her front door, and use my key to let myself in. I'm as quiet as a mouse as I sneak into the kitchen to try to find wine, or anything that will help ease the pain of losing Ellis.

Wine goes well with ice cream, doesn't it?

I open the fridge, and the kitchen light clicks on.

"What are you doing here? I almost called the police," my mother says, looking a bit frantic as she holds up a frying pan.

"Why would you call the police?" I grab the wine out of the fridge and shut the door.

"I thought you were an intruder." She glances at the clock. "What are you doing here so late?"

I hold up the bottle, my eyes tearing up. "I need wine." I move to the counter, trying my best not to completely melt-down. "Want some?"

My mother sets the frying pan down and steps closer. "Sure, why not."

I laugh a little, the humor keeping the tears from falling faster.

"Here let me." My mother takes the wine bottle from my hands and opens a drawer. "Sit down at the kitchen table and I'll bring you some."

I nod. Most people binge on chocolate. Me, I usually binge on ice cream. Most times I call the girls and we watch movies, but not this time. This time it feels more catastrophic and the only things a girl needs in times like these are her mother and wine. I watch each movement of my mother in her long pink robe, uncorking the bottle, and pouring us both a glass. I'm the product of divorce and don't get to see my father too often. But, let me say he missed out with having my mother around.

She has a way to calm and soothe without even saying a word. I know in the past she's been hard on me about getting married, but it's all part of who she is. A confident, competitive woman.

She sets the wine glass down in front of me, and I pick it up and take a sip, letting the cool buttery flavor fill my tongue of the Chardonnay.

"Thank you." I've nearly chugged half my glass, and my mother hasn't even touched hers.

"Rough day?"

"The roughest." I take another big gulp. "Ellis and I broke it off." I don't go into the details of Henry and him forcing me to do it, mainly because it's late and I am not feeling the full effects of my wine yet.

She rubs my back. "Oh no, that's horrible. He was such a great guy." I love the past tense. Like Ellis is no longer that great. Like it was his fault we're no longer together.

The first tear drops, just thinking about how great he is. "It just never would've worked. He lives there, I live here."

My mother stops rubbing my back and picks up her wine glass, taking a small sip. "Well, you're right this has been a rough night."

I laugh a little through the tears that are heavily falling now. "I know."

My mother, bless her heart, doesn't say anything, just hands me a box of tissues and takes another sip of her wine. We sit in silence for a few minutes, and it's exactly what I need right now. I finish off my glass of wine, and my mother fills another one for me.

"Kiki, you don't have to have your whole life figured out ahead of time. Hell," she laughs, "I'm still figuring mine out along the way." She wraps her arms around me, curling me into a hug.

"I know. I just so wanted to figure things out with him."

⊏⊐

I STAY at my mother's house and the next morning, I feel like
I've cried a river. My eyes are puffy, and I look like I was hit by a
Mack truck, and feel like it too.

"Morning," my mother singsongs, cooking something that
smells delicious on the stove. "Hope you're hungry."

I doubt I could eat, even though it all looks so delicious. I
make some sort of inaudible sound, and my mother shushes
it away.

"You need food." She places a plate in front of me, and I
smile at the eggs and bacon positioned in a smiley face for me.

"Mom, you do know I'm not five-years-old anymore, right?"

She smiles, leaning over to kiss my cheek. "I can spoil my
baby anytime she's here."

It's always good to come home, to remember where you
came from. Sure, I know my mother doesn't live too far away,
but I don't get home as much as I should. And that thought
saddens me.

"What are you doing today?" I ask my mother.

She shrugs. "Haven't really come up with anything. You?"

"I need to go to the Atwood's to collect all the decorations,
and make sure everything turned out ok." Leaving right in the
middle of the party I was throwing was probably not the best
idea. But, the party was dying down, and hopefully they don't
hold it against me. "I should get ready." I take a bite of the eggs,
and try my best to gather the courage of facing them.

Not so much the Atwood's, but Ellis. I hope he's not there.

Like I said, once the money is handled, and the deal goes
through then I know for a fact Ellis will be back on the first
flight to Georgia. It's sad, sure, but it's for the best.

Now their brewery will have the products I helped come up
with. Now every dog in America (ok the Southeast, until they
expand) can have a healthy doggy treat. That thought makes
me smile.

"Do you want me to go with you?" I love my mom.
"No, it'll be ok. I'm a big girl." Even though I don't feel like
it right now.

TWENTY-SIX

Ellis

NEVER TRUST THE HYPE...

"WHAT EXACTLY IS THAT?" I ask, rubbing out the crick in my neck from sleeping in my car. Yes, you heard that right. I slept in my car while waiting outside Kiki's house, in the mere hope I'd get to see her and try to understand why she said the words she did.

Is she right?

Is this whole thing going nowhere?

My life is in Atlanta, but I know she's my life now, too.

My brother draws back my attention when he clicks on the email. "It came this morning. From the Wright Brothers and Associates. Says they have no dealings with us."

I slam my fist on the desk. "What does this mean? Henry played us?"

Urban clicks the mouse, trying to back out of the email to

see if there's anything else explaining what's going on in his inbox. "I emailed their company a few days ago, just to make sure everything was on the up and up and we were ready to move forward. Ya know, because I was tired of Henry not committing to anything real."

"Right." Any time Urban or I asked Henry numbers and figures he always laughed and pushed it aside. Now I see we were taken for...what exactly? "It doesn't make sense."

"I know. We haven't signed any paperwork. We haven't given him anything. So, I'm not really sure what's going on." Urban stands from his chair. "I'm going down there."

"Well, I'm coming with you."

We hop in Urban's black SUV and head downtown to the Wright Brothers Investment Firm. If anyone can put an end to all the back and forth that we can never seem to get answers to, someone there can. Now that I'm thinking about it, Henry's been calling the shots and making sure no one knows which way is up or down.

"That man sure talks a good talk." I stare at my brother, wondering if he's realizing what I am.

"Yeah, like a con man."

The type of man to make you agree to anything he's asking you. A part of me wonders if that's why Kiki said yes to his proposal. I shake that thought away as quickly as it came. Henry is a player, in the worst kinds of way.

Not like how Urban plays around with women, but a different kind of player. A user. A kind that makes you believe every word that comes out of his mouth. Like, yes, he has the money to back every project we've ever needed to get done. "Are we stupid for believing this guy?" I ask him.

He shakes his head as he speeds through the streets. Like the faster he goes the more the truth won't sting. "No, he had the card. I'd heard of Wright Brothers. He said all the right things. Why wouldn't we believe him?"

"And we've known him for years," I say, relaxing a bit. This must be a mistake. Henry would never.

"Exactly."

"Yeah, he did everything right except cut the check." And that worries me.

I know Urban and I both have the same thing on our mind. The email better be a fake. The company better not be some sham of a thing, and Henry's ass better be there when we get there.

"Maybe you should call him," Urban says.

"No, he'll just talk us out of coming there today."

Urban nods, pulling the SUV into the parking lot of the firm. We both fly out, walking as quickly as we can without downright running. To make matters worse I keep checking my phone like a teenager to see if I've missed a call from Kiki. I haven't.

We burst through the doors like bank robbers ready for action, even though we're not here to take money but to find the money that was promised to us.

"May I help you," a busty blonde says at the entrance.

"We're here to see Mr. Wright." My brother smiles at me, like he's not even sure if the name is just a facade, or if there really are two brothers, last name Wright running the whole operation. "Do you have an appointment?"

Before we can even answer, we both spot Henry coming out of the elevator.

"Henry," I rush up to him, Urban right behind me, and the receptionist right behind him.

"Gentlemen, I'll have to have you make an appointment." She races after us, trying her best to halt our progress.

Henry turns, his eyes widening to the size of grapefruits, ok maybe not that big, and he stammers over his words, "Ellis, Urban, what are you doing here?" He checks his phone, most likely looking to see if we called before stopping by.

Another man comes out of his office and steps closer. "Henry, what's going on here?"

I can already see this whole scene escalating, and I take charge. "Sorry sir," I shake his hand, "we're clients of Henry's and we're just looking to meet with him to discuss some numbers."

The man appears utterly confused, like someone lost his cat. "Clients of Henry?"

"We're the owners of Bearded Goat Brewery, and have been working alongside Henry on an upcoming project that needs funding," I explain.

"Let's take this outside," Henry pleads, grabbing my arm and trying to lead us away.

The older man shakes his head. "But, Henry isn't an executive. He works in the mailroom."

This old man must be off his rocker for sure. "No, he's right here. In a suit." Mail guys don't wear suits, do they? No, not that I've ever seen.

The man laughs. "He's always wearing suits. It's part of his charm." The man sticks out his hand. "I'm Mr. Wright. I'm one of the owners here."

I shake his hand, because if I don't I'll use this hand to punch Henry instead. "Nice to meet you, sir." And then Urban shakes his hand, introducing us both.

I can't stop staring at Henry, trying my best to figure out what exactly is going on. Mailroom?

"I'm sorry for the confusion gentlemen, but make an appointment with Charlene. I'd love to discuss your brewery with you."

I shake his hand again, thanking him.

Urban steps up to Charlene's desk as I walk outside with Henry.

"Let me explain." He holds his hands up in a mock surrender pose. "I planned on backing you guys. I did. I thought if maybe I brought your ideas to my boss it would help us all out. You'd get your money, I'd get my promotion."

I shake my head. "Henry, this isn't a game. We trusted you, and you let us down."

"Did Kiki tell you? Is that why you're here?"

"Tell me what?" Kiki knew this man was a lying sack of shit?

"About our deal."

"What deal?" I step closer to Henry and he backs up.

Urban walks out of the building and stands beside me. "What's he saying?"

"Says Kiki and he had some sort of deal going on." I'm ready to knock the shit out of this guy, but I'm not an idiot. I'm also not a teenager and can control my anger. I know you punch someone and you are costing yourself a lifetime of regret. Possible jail time. Being sued, and Henry looks the type to sue someone for that kind of thing. So, I resist, even though it'd feel so fucking good.

"Start talking," Urban says, folding his arms across his chest.

"Well, as I was telling her I like to win," Urban and I exchange a look, "and well, I figured if we'd be working together it would be in her best interest not to be involved with you."

I see flames.

"And in contretemps, I'd rather not be working with someone who is dating my ex. So, it all works out now."

Is this guy on drugs?

"But we're *not* working together," Urban says. "You work in the mailroom."

"Semantics." He shrugs a cocky shoulder.

I take a deep breath in, to control the anger coursing through my veins at a very rapid pace. "You told Kiki to break up with me?"

"Not in so many words."

I step closer and Henry backs away like a frightened little

pig. "Look I don't care about Kiki. Just put in a good word with my boss, please." And now he's reduced to begging.

"You're a sack of shit."

Urban and I walk away, wanting nothing to do with Henry or his firm.

"We could still meet with the investors," Urban says, driving back to the brewery.

I shrug. "There's really no point." And maybe I'll feel better in a few days, but right now my mind is only on one thing. Kiki.

And Kiki alone.

"I have something to handle when I get back. What are you going to do?" I ask Urban.

"Dad wanted to see us both. Do you want to see him first?"

Of course, I don't. But, of course I will. "Sure."

And afterward, I'm running to Kiki's.

On foot if I have to.

To straighten out this whole mess.

TWENTY-SEVEN

Kiki

NEVER TRUST YOUR FRIENDS...

IT'S BEEN three whole days since I last saw Ellis, and I'm sure by now he's back in Atlanta living his best single life. I've been in a cocoon that consists of work, ice cream, and binge-watching *Outlander* on Netflix. To say I've rarely seen the outside is an understatement.

But, today, Lola has somehow once again been able to draw me from my very own fortress of solitude and cast me out into the world on another fitness escapade. I do it because I love her.

I actually do it because she threatened if I didn't she would be sure to post the video of my karaoke singing on her blog that gets over one-million views.

I don't need that level of humiliation right now.

She says I'm not the best singer, but to me...I'm Adele.

No, I'm Celine Dion. Well, I'm whoever is singing the song

I'm listening to and I sound just like them. Trust me, I sing right on key. (which key that is, I have no idea.)

"What are we doing today? Bungee jumping while doing Pilates in the air?"

Lola smiles. "No, but that's a great idea." She waits for Poppi to join us before telling us what we'll be doing in today's little misadventure in exercising. "Today we're doing a simple karaoke singing and rave."

"I don't know if I can really bounce around today." I just don't have the energy to sing and dance.

"I know you're a little blue but trust me." Poppi winks. "You need this today."

I roll my eyes. "Fine, but only because I know you girls love my killer dance moves."

Both Poppi and Lola try not to laugh as we step inside the dance studio. It's bigger than expected with a stage near the front of the room. There's a karaoke machine and microphone on stage, and I set my water bottle and towel in the back of the room next to Poppi's.

Lola stretches. "This is going to be great. And I need to make sure I get lots of good footage for my blog." She takes out her iPhone and gets it ready.

The instructor comes in with a wide smile. "Everyone ready to bust a move and get their sing on?" Why is every fitness instructor so full of energy?

It's seven in the morning, people.

I do a little stretch and get ready to dance. I love dancing, even if people think I don't dance well. I know the real truth, they're just jealous.

"Let's get moving," the instructor calls out.

Lola and Poppi rush to get onto the dancefloor, and I follow closely behind.

"Is that Bon Jovi?" I ask Poppi as the beginning notes of "Living On A Prayer" blast through the speakers. And then I see him, Ellis, strolling across the stage until he's in front of the microphone.

He sings the opening lyrics, "Once upon a time not so long ago."

I smile, keeping my eyes on him as he belts out the next line. And let me just say something right now...this man can *not* sing. Like oh my god, bad.

He can't carry a tune to save his life.

And it's a-fucking-dorable.

Everyone cheers. Of course, they do, because that's what you do when a gorgeous man gets up on stage and sings his ever-loving heart out for the woman he wants.

And oh my god, that woman is me.

Chills erupt across my skin as he keeps singing, bending his knees to get the right amount of angst in each note.

He even sings the lyrics wrong, "It doesn't make a difference if we're naked or not."

He points to me, calling me up on stage with him. I laugh, shaking my head back and forth.

"Do it. Go," Poppi says, pushing me closer to the stage.

The instructor hands me a microphone as I make my way closer to him. I can't stop smiling. I read the words on the screen, singing out the next line, "Woah, livin' on a prayer."

Poppi and Lola cheer as Ellis' face erupts into a smile. And then he and I sing the rest of the song out together, and I have to say...I sound just like Bon Jovi.

━━

"WELL, you have one thing in common," Poppi says after the class is over. "Neither of you can dance, *or* sing worth a damn."

Ellis wraps me into his arms. "I sing great. It's this one here," he snuggles me closer, "who was throwing my groove off."

I laugh. "Never."

We wave Lola and Poppi off, and I turn to face him. "How did you know I was here?"

"I called the Spaw, and talked to Poppi. Told her all about what Henry did, and she told me you'd be here."

"I'm sorry about Henry. I should have told him to fuck off, but I couldn't be the reason you lost the brewery."

Ellis studies me for a moment. "We're not going to lose it. But, more on that later. And, get this, it's not because of Henry." He steps closer. "Did you know Henry was a mail boy?"

"A what?"

"Yeah, he wasn't even an investor over at the firm. He worked in the mailroom."

I can't believe my ears. "No way." Now I feel even worse. "I'm so sorry I ever fell for his bullshit."

Ellis sets his hands on my hips. "It's ok. He duped us too. He's one of those kinds of guys. The kind that can sell ice to an Eskimo. It's a great quality to have. He just doesn't use it very well."

I nod. "I'll say." And I think back to my relationship with Henry. Was it all one big manipulation?

It doesn't matter now, because right here and right now, I have the man.

I have the one I've always wanted.

And even though we don't have all the answers, I know that together we can make it all work out.

They say, never kiss a stranger...but never say never.

222

Epilogue

Ellis

NEVER TAKE LIFE FOR GRANTED...

NOW THAT IS something I can actually agree with. I knew I'd win Kiki back the moment she walked away from me. I just didn't know the when or how of it all.

I knew she needed time. What I didn't know at the time was that Henry had forced her not to date me.

He'd filled her head with lies, and she fell for the bait. Can't say that I blame her though, to save her company I'd probably do it too.

Cause there's nothing I wouldn't do for this woman.

The brewery is finally turning around, and the new products are being well received. See, there's something I never thought would happen. Like never in a million years did I guess the old man would sell off almost everything he owns to fund his own brewery, and help his sons get back on their feet.

Listen, I haven't said I've forgiven the man, but I'm getting closer. Like the olive branch is extending closer, and maybe one day soon I'll take hold.

I can say one thing, the man sure is trying hard.

And maybe I've been a little too harsh on him.

Yes, after I sang my heart out to get the girl back, I never left. That's right, you are looking at Jupiter's newest resident. I begged my mother to come down too, but she was happy I was moving down, and said she'd be down for the wedding and then smiled, like she knew it'd happen sooner than I think it will.

Like I said, I'm not opposed to marriage, and when I do get married it'll be to the hottest babe in South Florida.

We left the distribution office in good hands in Atlanta, and I was able to move down in a heartbeat.

Which is a good thing, because I don't know if I'd be able to survive without this girl by my side.

"Are you almost ready?" Kiki calls from the living room of my new condo.

"Almost." I meet her by the door, kissing her cheek because I can. "What should we sing tonight?" Yes, Kiki and I have become quite the karaoke aficionados. In fact, we've been able to turn a crowd into a frenzy with our hot dance moves and killer vocals.

AFTER THE CLUB, I hold her hand in the parking lot, walking her to my car. Before she gets inside, I wrap my arms around her, folding her into my chest and kissing her, letting my tongue explore hers.

I'm sporting the biggest hard on in history right now and it's all thanks to Kiki's little outfit she's got on. It accentuates all the right things. Legs. Tits. Ass.

She opens the back door and pulls me inside on a moan. Her sweet coconut-smelling skin has me craving to go further south. To the parts of her body I'm yearning for. Parts I've been dreaming of all day while at work.

Because everything I'm craving is beneath her dress. It's cramped in the backseat, but I'll make do. I slide down her body, and when I reach her thighs, I lift her dress with my teeth, until it's up and off. I'm met with her white-lace bra as I glide my fingers around her back to unsnap it.

"Wow. That was impressive," she says as I remove her bra.

"It's not the only thing I'm good at, trust me."

She laughs a soft laugh, and I'm enamored with the swell of her breasts and the pink nipples begging me to taste them in the darkness.

And I do. I suck one into my mouth, letting my tongue run over her hard nipple as my hand massages the other one.

I fucking want her.

The fire is stoked.

It's blazing my skin.

Making me burn for more.

My vision blurring.

I'm teetering on the edge.

Her body syncs with mine as we grind against each other. I need to taste her. Her panties are damp, and next thing I know they're off, flying through the air.

This is some sort of exquisite torture, and I know I can't take it anymore.

I fling her leg over my shoulder and drag my tongue down her smooth skin to what I want more than anything.

I groan, letting her scent fill my nostrils. She's so fucking wet. And so fucking tight as I slip a finger inside her. And then another.

I lower my mouth onto her, sucking her sweet taste and savoring it on my tongue. Her hands make tunnels and pathways in my hair, and I keep licking and tasting every inch of her pussy. I'm drunk on her. And there's no AA class I could take to ever want me to give this up.

I reach my hands around and squeeze her ass, gripping her hot flesh, my fingers digging in.

"Oh god, Ellis," she cries out, making my dick ache. Making it pulse uncontrollably. But, I won't think about my own release right now.

I have more important things to do.

"You like when I suck on your clit?" I ask the question, but knowing full well she loves it. Because she goes wild. She goes crazy with lust.

I take a quick peek, watching her eyes squeeze shut as she arches her back in ecstasy. She's on the brink of coming, and I release her ass to plunge two fingers inside her.

Her thighs close in, keeping me in place as she pants for me not to stop.

My heart's raging against my chest as I keep kissing and sucking her clit between my lips.

I swear, this girl does things to me.

Everything fades away as Kiki comes crashing down around me from her orgasm. It really is something quite amazing, and I memorize the sound.

As soon as she's calmed, I kiss up her stomach and gaze into her eyes, noticing how right after her orgasm they lighten just a shade. "You're so fucking hot," I tell her.

"And you're so fucking mine," she says back.

And she's telling the truth.

I am forever hers. Never in a million years did I think I'd get this lucky, but...*never say never.*

ENJOYED KIKI AND ELLIS? Stay tuned for Lola and Urban's love story coming soon in: NEVER DATE A PLAYER

CLICK HERE to sign up for updates on when Never Date A Player releases.

Sneak Peek of Cold Hearted Baller

Calliope

My veins are going to explode. I scan the list of ingredients in the Max Energy drink I consumed this morning, checking to see if drugs are listed. They aren't.

With a move I imagine is worthy of Maxwell Hunter, the star pitcher who endorses it, I wind my arm back and rocket the sleek silver can across the conference room of Mayhem Marketing. It thunks against the cream-colored wall and lands with a thump inside the small trash can.

"Yesss," I exclaim as the door opens.

"They're ready for you, Calliope," Rita, assistant to the man who's going to hire me to cater all of his marketing company's functions, informs me with a furrowed brow.

He hasn't actually agreed to hire me yet, but he will, because according to the energy drink 'It's winning in a can.'

"Let's do this, Rita," I nearly squeal, ping-ponging around the room where I'll be serving the King and his court various items I've created. "I'm going to win them over with my baking skills."

"You ok?" she asks, at half the speed I seem to be talking.

I give her two very animated thumbs up, feeling like my arms are going to shoot off to the ceiling.

"Yes." I smooth my hands down the long length of my hair, from root to bottom. The usually heavy brown locks feel like they're standing on end. I need to calm down, but I can't. I feel electrified. Times one hundred.

She moves to the corner of the room as Tobias Longwood, grey-haired owner of Mayhem Marketing, enters, followed by two men in suits. My heart rate accelerates to an unnatural rhythm. I'm not sure if it's the energy drink or the fact I've been dreaming about this opportunity for such a long time. If I can land this account, I'll finally have the extra money to expand my cafe. Thanks to Max Energy, that thought makes me extra excited.

"Miss Thomas, hello," Tobias greets me. "Thanks for coming."

"Nice to meet you," I respond a little too loud over the pulse in my ears, giving his outstretched hand several vigorous pumps.

His brow furrows just like Rita's did, and I try to dial it down a notch, but my dial is broken.

It can't be normal that my lips tingle when I smile as Tobias introduces me to the two execs who will help decide my fate about whether or not I'll be hired.

While the people I'm here to impress take a seat at the rectangular table, I chatter, uncontrollably, about my creations and with jittery hands remove the rich chocolate cake adorned with the Mayhem logo from its box.

"Looks delicious," Tobias compliments me as I move closer at warp speed.

My feet walk faster than my heels can keep up, and instead of placing my showpiece in the center of the table, the cake somehow teeters amidst a chorus of gasps to end up a ganache mess... right in Tobias' lap. All three layers.

"I'm so sorry," I apologize, staring at the broken lump on his groin.

"Are you on drugs?" he asks with a pinched face, looking down at the red Mayhem logo smeared on his pristine white shirt.

"No," I deny, "I can explain." My eyes dart at a rapid pace to the shocked expressions on the other faces seated at the table.

"You get one shot here. That was yours. Thank you for coming in, Miss Thomas."

"It was an energy drink—Max Energy—by that famous baseball player," I tell him, because like he said, this is my one shot. "Listen, whoever marketed that as success in a can should be fired."

As he removes a lump of cake from his soiled trousers into the garbage can Rita retrieved, he informs me, "We designed that campaign."

The room is silent as I pack my things and go. All of my dreams follow me out the door. I'm too high on Max Energy to be depressed.

I have no one to blame but myself. And Maxwell Hunter, the man behind the drink.

When I get home, I drop my purse on the kitchen counter and beeline straight for the fridge. MyOn the top shelf, next to the milk, sit the remaining cans of Max Energy. I tilt one of the tall cylinders and read the tiny black font:

Max Energy will give you that extra you need to reach your goals. It's winning in a can.

Share your success.

Leave a review.

The words taunt me before I toss it in the trash. The four cans left in my fridge follow it into the garbage before I move over to my laptop on the island in my kitchen. I type in the web address to the Nile site listed on the can and search for Max Energy, clicking on the tiny thumbnail, and then, scrolling through all the five star reviews.

Delicious! I finished a project for work that earned me a bonus.

Homerun. Finally, put together the bookshelf I'd been dreading.

Review after review raves about this drink.

7 stars!

I'd give it 100 if I could! I've never tasted anything like this or had so much energy. You will love it!

Seven out of five?

I can barely refrain from commenting to ReviewQueen that her rating is impossible. You can *not* give more than you have.

I click on 'My Review' and select one star. Annoyance flows through my veins and spills out from my fingertips as I type.

Let me share my story with you. It doesn't have a happy ending, just like the book I had stayed up all night reading didn't. I was tired the next morning, and my coworker had given me these from her PR package, so I thought, 'Sure, I'll try it.' I drank one before the most important meeting of my life. Big mistake.

This is not success in a can. Don't drink the kool aid, people. Or actually, do. Maybe you won't bounce off the walls and lose your dream client. Thanks, Max. Thank you for my failure. I hope you have a losing season.

And then, I press the submit button. Take that, Maxwell Hunter.

CLICK HERE to read more! Available in Kindle Unlimited.

Sneak Peek of Cold Hearted Bastard

Olivia

Five Things. That's the title of tonight's video I'm watching. More like salivating over. Each day, a social media coordinator picks a fireman from the Hightower Hills Fire Department to interview and she asks him 'five things' about himself that the community may not know. There are nine other videos of different men on the playlist, but I keep rewinding back to the man of my desire—Corbin Carmack.

I'm watching these videos like he might let a secret slip out. Something special that could get me closer to him. Something that would whisper into my ears the key to unlocking his heart. Silly, right?

If you asked me five things about myself that people may not know, it would go a little something like this:

1. I love a man with brown eyes.

2. I've never wanted a stranger as much as I do him.

3. I'm going to extremes that could get me tossed in jail just to steal glimpses of him.

4. For the last two months I've blown off friends, family, and

everything in between to stay up late at night and watch this video as I pleasure myself to sleep.

5. I set my house on fire to meet him.

Well wait, let me explain...

I first saw Corbin when he made national news, rescuing my neighbor's baby boy from their burning house in the Cedar Crest subdivision where I live. Charlotte—said baby boy's mom — screamed from their front lawn, while her husband, Thomas, clutched her in his arms as she begged for him to let her go, because their son was still trapped inside.

With the heat threatening to scorch my skin from where I stood behind the safety of the barricades, I watched in awe as Corbin leapt from the blaring fire engine and charged right into the flames of Hell without a second thought. Even with the protective gear he was wearing, I couldn't imagine being that fearless, that daring. But *he* was.

After a few heart-stopping moments, Corbin emerged from the burning house with Benjamin clutched to him. His mask covered the baby's face to give him oxygen, while he sucked smoke, and the selfless act hit me right in the heart. And the vagina.

Everyone stood in their pajamas and robes applauding his rescue, and I'm sure, afterward, like *normal* people, went back to sleep. Went back to living their lives.

I must be strange, or deranged, because the first thing I did that night was look up the heroic rescuer to find out his name. All the information was right there online. His name, phone number, address—hell, even his *email* address. The internet also told me his family member's names, and while I had a lot of trouble finding anyyyyything about Corbin on Facebook, his mom has a penchant for posting every single thing about herself. Her name is Greta, and she loves cooking, fishing, and Jesus. From her numerous posts, it would appear in that exact order.

But then, I looked up the Hightower Hills Instagram account and was bombarded with videos, live feeds, and pictures galore. It was like my very own personal oasis of Corbin-candy. I devoured every video, deciding on the 'five things' one as my favorite, and saved every picture of Corbin to my phone. The word stalker has nothing on me.

And this is why I'm beginning to unravel. This is why I'm going to drastic measures to get close to him. I can't take it anymore. He's consuming my every single thought.

I wake with him on my brain. I go to sleep with him still there. On my fingertips that wander down into the hem of my panties when I should be getting a full night's sleep so I can wake in the morning fully refreshed and ready to teach a class-room full of kindergarteners.

Ugh. See? Deranged. I'm supposed to set an example for the next generation, and here I am breaking laws and moral codes. I'm hunting this person down and trying to dig into their life because I have a sick need to get closer to a total stranger.

I know that we'll never be together—in love—or any kind of real relationship. In reality, when I step back and think about what I've done, I know it's wrong. But when I study him on the screen, all I see is a man that I want to be his everything. I want him to look into my eyes and fuck me raw. I want his sweet nothings in the morning. I want him holding me in bed with his strong tattooed arms, smelling like smoke and fire.

Ah shit, the smoke alarm is going off. My lungs are starting to fight. Oh god, what have I done?

I can't just walk up to the firehouse, introduce myself, and offer me up as some kind of prize. So, I've done all my research and I know what he likes. I've sat and watched from across the street, parked at the post office, as he picks up an order from Rosario's Italian Delicatessen every Friday. I know every morning at five-thirty he's at the gym. He runs treadmill first, then weights, then back to the treadmill. At eight forty-five, he likes to stop at JoJo Juice and order a mix of pomegranate, cherry, kale, and pineapple after his workout.

Oh, no. Oops. I started a full on fire.

"911, what is your emergency?"

"Yes, my name is..." I choke, "...Olivia Poppins. I need help. There's a fire in my kitchen." The red flames rise higher, spreading across the white cabinets. I race to the front of the house and lie on the cool tile near the door. My heart races inside my chest. "Please, send help."

Like I said, I've never done anything like this in my life, and never dreamt that I would, but my obsession is beating my brains, and I won't rest until I can feel him inside me.

I try to make it to my front door, but the flames rise higher and higher. Oh no, what have I done?

They say when you die you're supposed to see a white light, hear angels singing and be reunited with your loved ones—the good ones who made it into Heaven, anyway.

Not me. When *I* died, all I saw was a sea of blue. And I'm not talking about the ocean or skyline. Nope. More like, the navy blue shirts of Hightower Hills paramedic crew pounding my chest until my ribs protested under the pressure of their mighty fists pumping with fervor to resuscitate me.

This was *not* the uber romantic rescue of my dreams where a scorching hot fireman—Corbin Carmack—swoops in to lift me up into his strong tattooed arms before carrying me to safety.

There was no surrounding my mouth with his succulent man lips as he breathed his superhero oxygen into my lungs.

Not even a standard 'he kissed me awake' like a fairytale princess rescue.

Nada. Squat.

Instead, a bald man named Edgar put his sour-tasting mouth to mine and blew air into my lungs until I choked and nearly vomited on him. To make matters worse, I've been labeled the woman who *almost* died heating up chocolate sauce. That's the story I told them. They don't need to know I was trying to have the sexiest fireman in the world come to my rescue.

I've never tried to set a fire before. Hell, I wasn't even trying to set a fire *tonight*. I figured a little dramatic smoke and a helpless damsel in distress would be enough. But apparently, ha, chocolate burns really, *really* fast.

I try to sit up, even though my chest is also on fire. Edgar urges me to lie back down, but I shove away from him and attempt to make my way back to my house. I'm doing fine on my feet, until I reach my mailbox and the whole world begins to tilt sideways. I reach for the metal box to steady myself but slip and stumble forward into a hard wall.

But walls don't talk.

"Whoa. Hold on there. Where do you think you're going, Miss Pyro?"

Lord Jesus, take me now. It's him.

His voice. His arms. His smell.

Everything I've been fantasizing about for months is all around me. But, this is not how I planned for it to go.

I want to shove away and hide myself, but I can't escape. I'm wobbly on my feet and he holds me fast with warm hands on my hips. His upper arms brush the sides of my breasts. I finally brave glancing up into his face and he smiles down at me, his teeth super white against the backdrop of tan skin and dark scruff. He's even more beautiful and heartbreaking in person than he was in those videos.

"M-my name is Poppins," I stammer, locked on his caramel eyes.

"Well, tonight, you're Little Miss Pyro." He nods his head toward my house. "Burned down half your kitchen. Is this how you usually spend a Friday night alone?"

"I was making fondue," I lie.

His hands stay on my hips, eyes on mine. His tongue licks over his bottom lip before he says, "Too bad you burned it. Hot date planned tonight?"

I beam back at him. "Is that a firefighter joke?"

Instead of answering my poor attempt to flirt, he props his arm under mine as a crutch, and tries to walk with me in his hold, but I sway a bit. "Sorry, I'm a little…"

Before I can finish my sentence, he swoops me up and carries me easily in his arms back to the ambulance. I pretty much want to die. But also, I'm swooning like a Swoony McSwoonster. Silently, of course.

"Hey, Edgar," he says, bouncing me ever so slightly, "I think you lost something."

"No. She ran away," Edgar huffs. "I'm a year away from retirement and not in the damn mood to be running people down who don't want my help."

"Understood," Corbin says, glancing at me with a glint of wickedness in his eyes and then back to Edgar. "But as long as you're still on the payroll, you got a fucking job to do."

The old man folds his arms. "Not until she apologizes."

"I think she needs to save her air for something more useful than stroking your ego." Corbin turns away from Edgar and heads to the fire engine, placing me on the silver platform on the back. He retrieves two blue blankets from a compartment.

"They had to split your dress down the middle, because they thought they might need to use paddles on you."

He glances down to my chest, and I follow his line of vision and see that I've had my white semi-see-through bra on display the entire time. My cheeks flush as he wraps the soft fleece around my shoulders.

"You should stay warm so you don't go into shock."

He rubs up and down my arms, and if he doesn't stop doing that, I'm going to need the hose turned on me to put out the fire igniting deep in my bones.

"I am," I say, hypnotized by his soul-stirring eyes.

"Hmm?" He continues massaging my arms and now a little over my back as he makes circles around my shoulders. Good god. I'm gonna need more than a fire hose spraying me down if he doesn't quit that.

"What?" I ask.

He laughs. "You said 'I am.' I'm trying to figure out what 'you are.'"

"I…" am your stalker. In love with a stranger. Want to pounce on you. Watch you every night while pleasuring myself. A complete (harmless, except to myself) psycho that's having an internet romance with you, without you knowing it.

Best to avoid truths in this answer, so I stall with stuttering over animal noises and incomplete sentences until another man approaches us. His pristine white shirt grabs Corbin's attention. It's the Battalion Chief. I know this because I've watched his 'Five Things' video too, hoping there might be some footage of Corbin in it. Sadly, there wasn't. He's a former New York smoke sucker, and he wears it proudly in his thick accent and swagger. The chief has Edgar in tow.

"Seems there's a mix up between who's s'posta be putting out fires and who is s'posta be takin' fire-starters to the hospital," the Chief says.

"Miss," Edgar says hard, but looking fearful of the chief, "please come with me."

Corbin offers me his hand and I contemplate for a second before I allow myself to feel him. My hand slides into his—slow —so I can brace for whatever spark ignites. They do not burst into flames on contact like I expected, but I'm going to hope he felt a flicker of something.

He's rough to the touch, but gentle, as he pulls me to my feet and leads me over to Edgar. "Got her?" he asks, not letting me go yet.

Edgar nods, but I doubt he could catch me if I stumbled. He's half Corbin's size, in every way you slice it.

I look back at Corbin. "Thank you."

He smiles that smile I've watched for months, complete with

the signature dimple in the pocket of his left cheek. "Unless you want me to come back here, Miss Pyro, stay away from fondue."

Stay away? I almost killed myself getting you to come.

Ha.

That's what she said.

I stare up at him. "You can rescue me anytime you like, Mr. Carmack. You're like my white knight."

He laughs. "Please, call me Corbin. And I'll pencil your rescues in." Did he just wink at me?

This is going better than expected. In fact, I say by this time next year you'll be able to hear wedding bells.

"Until we meet again," I say as Edgar carts me away.

"Don't go starting any more fires, Little Miss Pyro."

I wave and then turn around, happy with the way things worked out. I'm pretty sure I have some serious insta-love for the guy.

Setting my house on fire? Totally worth it.

CLICK HERE to continue reading! Now available in Kindle Unlimited.

Acknowledgments

With the world a mess right now, it was very hard for me to keep my funny going while writing this book. I'd like to thank everyone in my Logan Chance's The Dark Side Facebook Group for keeping my sanity in check, and by keeping spirits up. CLICK HERE to join!

I'd also like to thank Paula Dawn for all her help in bringing this story to life. I appreciate all your help, and thank you. You truly looked out for Kiki and Ellis, and I hope you feel better soon.

Thank you to Valerie and Vanessa for reading this book at a moments notice. I truly appreciate it.

Thank you to the hardest working pimpers out there, and all the members of my Logang. You ladies rock and I couldn't ask for a better team.

I truly appreciate all the bloggers who share my work. You all are truly an inspiration, and I appreciate your generosity. Thank you.

Thank you so much to Jennifer and Danielle with Wildfire Marketing Solutions for helping me out with this release.

Jennifer, thank you for answering all my questions, and I appreciate your help.

Silver Book Tours, thank you Maia for all your enthusiasm and hard work.

Thank you to anyone who has ever taken a chance on me, I truly appreciate your dedication, and thank you for making my dreams a reality.

To my readers, you are the reason I do what I do, and I appreciate every single like, share, mention, review, purchase, post, and every and all things. Thank you so much.

About the Author

Logan Chance is a USA Today and Top 20 Amazon Bestselling Author with a quick wit and penchant for the simple things in life: Star Wars, music, and smart girls who love to read. He was nominated best debut author for the Goodreads Choice Awards in 2016. His works can be classified as Dramedies (Drama+Comedies), featuring a ton of laughs and many swoon worthy, heartfelt moments.

Also by Logan Chance

The Playboy Series
PLAYBOY
HEARTBREAKER
STUCK
LOVE DOCTOR

The Me Series
DATE ME
STUDY ME
SAVE ME
BREAK ME

Sexy Standalones
TAKEN
WE ALL FALL DOWN
THE NEWLYFEDS
GRAHAM

Steamy Duets
THE DECEIT DUET
THE BOSS DUET

The Cold Hearted Series
COLD HEARTED BALLER

COLD HEARTED BASTARD

Box Sets

A VERY MERRY ALPHA CHRISTMAS

ME: THE COMPLETE SERIES

FAKE IT BABY ONE MORE TIME